CHRISTMAS MAGIC

A Time Bubble Novella

SAMANTHA JACOBEY

Lavish
Publishing LLC

First Edition

2019 Lavish Publishing, LLC

All Rights Reserved

Published in the United States by Lavish Publishing, LLC, Midland, TX

Cover Design by: Victor R. Sosa

Cover Images: CanStock Photo

Paperback Edition

ISBN: 978-1-944985-83-7

www.LavishPublishing.com

Contents

DEPARTMENT OF HISTORICAL Research
December 8, 2084

Taking the steps at the central control building in twos, Nathaniel Crabtree tucked his personal device into an inner pocket on his jacket. He had pulled it out several times on his stroll to Paul Hidalgo's office and couldn't wait to show him his find. Entering the large glass doors, he offered a nod to the security officer on the ground floor and made his way to the elevators.

"This is going to be big," he mumbled with a grin as he pushed the button to the lift. He had hardly slept the night before in anticipation and had doubled his workout that morning to clear some of his nervous energy. *I'm not sure it helped,* he considered as he paced in wait, then stepped back as the doors opened.

Once the carriage had emptied, he trotted on board and pushed the button for floor ninety-two. "Hi," he greeted the few who joined him in the small space, rubbing his hands together with excitement as the elevator closed and began its ascent.

Nathan had been an analyst for the department of historical research nigh on twenty years and was preparing for his annual jaunt into the past. For his new project and exposé, he had chosen a unique, if not controversial period to study. As an added twist, he had located a specific target to shadow; one that could be difficult to get approved, but he intended to try. *This year is special,* he thought to himself, having felt so ever since he discovered the well-preserved treasure and clue he hoped to investigate.

Paul had been his control for the last five of his missions, and although he had never disallowed any of them, he had always proven more problematic than his predecessor when assessing the details. As usual, Nate had done all the legwork to prepare his files and flight plan. He had researched the location he intended to bubble and secured the stop and start dates. *That part's going to be tricky for sure.*

The doors opening before him, he heaved a deep sigh, shaking his hands gently to relax his nerves as he strutted down the hall. Arriving at the waiting area, he grinned down at the shapely blond receptionist, who monitored visitors for that section of the floor and the few control agent offices that it held. "Hello, Dianna."

"Hi, Nate." She smiled sweetly, taking in his broad shoulders and well-kept physique. "Paul had a meeting but should return shortly," she informed him, indicating a row of chairs along the wall.

"I'll be fine," he agreed, not sure if it were true. Today, he might go stark raving mad at any moment. Taking one of the upholstered cushions, he leaned back into the seat and pulled out his small handheld computer. Lighting the screen, he perused the itinerary he would propose, stopping briefly to study the headstone once more. *Not bad for over three hundred years old,* he silently observed, as the marker had weathered well over the centuries.

Grazing the image with his thumb, he considered again what the young woman might have looked like. *Two years younger than me,* he observed for the umpteenth time. Gwendolyn had become an obsession since he found the hunk of sandstone, but he couldn't let on as much. He had to play it cool if he was to gain permission to travel back and see her in the flesh.

"Nathan?" Paul's stern voice startled him, snapping the analyst back to the present.

"Hi, Paul." He beamed, getting to his feet and offering his hand for a firm shake. "I've laid everything out just the way you like it," he cajoled as he followed the shorter man into his office.

"I'm sure you did." The control agent chuckled. Fifty on his last birthday, Paul had overseen thousands of jumps since the program was started but had never actually time traveled himself. Something in the idea of being converted to energy and transported through the bubble made him queasy. However, since it was his job to ensure that all the analysts under him had safe trips, he took that role very seriously.

"We don't want any accidents," he chided gently as he sank into his large leather chair, "so you'll have to bear with me while I check your details." A short man with a stocky build and pudgy middle, Paul took every opportunity to assert his position over his subordinates, especially the one before him with his tall frame and well-toned muscles.

"Of course." Nathaniel grinned, presenting his device for inspection before taking a seat across from him.

Lighting it, Paul started with the travel documents, noting the dates. "The American Revolution. Nice. That's a bit of a hot topic these last few years."

"Yes, sir," Nate agreed, gently chewing the side of his right thumb. *I'm going to die if I don't get this one.*

Still flipping through the screens, the control agent paused, examining one of them closely. "Thirty-eight years? That's a bit specific, isn't it? Not to mention long."

"Yes, sir." Nate nodded, tapping his left hand

against the arm of the chair. "But it's still well within limits."

Arriving at the last page of the proposal, Paul glared at the image. "Gwendolyn Romano," he read, noting the dates beneath her name. "Thirty-eight years. Nathan, you realize you're not allowed to target specific subjects without an S-fifty-three clearance."

"Oh, yes, sir," Nathan squirmed. "I'm not really focusing on the woman. I just thought it would give me a nice backdrop for the exposé. I don't really intend to meet her for an interview, so the S-fifty-three won't really be necessary."

"But you've targeted two very specific points in her life, her first and last Christmas," Paul bit tartly.

"Yes, well, that's only a few weeks from now, so I thought it would be appropriate. I don't really have a family, so Christmas isn't a magical time of year for me. It's just another day, and no one will miss me around here. Besides, the demand on the portals should be a bit freer on account of the holiday, and I can have a special blind constructed since I'll be there for such an extended period."

Seeing the other man had not been convinced, judging by his grimace, he gushed on, "And, the target location is on the Astrid family estate, which means I should have an opportunity to observe her, or at least learn of her over the course of the jump. I've researched it carefully and given you every detail." Waving a hand to indicate the device his boss still held, Nathan practically begged, "Please, sir. This one is important to me."

Raising his eyes to study the analyst before him, Paul leaned back in his chair. Using his index finger to smooth his greying beard over his chin, he asked quietly, "Why is that?"

Faltering, Nathaniel shrugged. "I've been at this a long time. I started straight out of college, when things were just getting interesting. I write a new exposé every year, and with each one, I feel like I have to one up the last. You know... stay ahead of the pack so to speak."

"And you think following this woman will get you an edge?"

"I have no idea." Nate laughed with a deep rumble. "What I do know is that she lived almost perfectly within the dates of the American Revolution. She died fairly young, and there is little record of her life available even though her name suggests ties to one of the wealthiest families of the time period in that area."

"I see." His control grinned. "And you think this is your chance to discover some lost piece of history."

"Exactly!" Nate near shouted, poking a single digit into the air. "I mean, everyone loves Ben Franklin, but he's been done. Overdone, if you ask me. I want to tackle someone fresh. And a woman in that era, that's a story that simply has to be told."

Pursing his lips, Paul considered the request for a full minute, noting that the man across from him hardly took a breath as he waited. Finally, he held out the personal device and stated calmly, "You'll need to make the necessary arrangements through the sixth-floor access. Eight has been giving us random feedback, so it will be down for a diagnostic for the next few weeks. Taking advantage of that holiday you mentioned," he added with a grin.

"You mean I get to go?" Nate whispered, hardly able to believe his ears.

"Yes, you get to go." Paul chuckled. "It still amazes me a forty-year-old man can be so wide eyed about these things."

Laughing with glee, Nathan took no insult at the words. "Thank you, sir," he coughed as he got to his feet and left the office before his control had a chance to change his mind.

ONE

A Star in the Night

COTTAGE OUTPOST
December 24th, 1760 – year 1

"Wow, what a beautiful sky!" Nathan observed, his eyes shifting as he craned his neck to admire the view through a wide window. Arriving at a new location always made him euphoric, and this jump even more so.

Above the line of trees, the darkness was littered with shimmering points of light, far more than could be seen from pretty much anywhere on earth in the year he had come from. Across the ground, a white blanket of snow gave a post-card quality to the scene, and the crescent moon added just the right amount of light. *There's some Christmas magic,* he mocked, not really a believer of such things.

Inhaling deeply, he sighed, "Air's cleaner, too."

Although there had been many strides made to clear the atmosphere since the third world war, the silent war as it was commonly called, he could feel the difference in his lungs. Dropping the curtain and shaking his head to remove the disturbing recent history, he prepared to delve into the past, and his current assignment.

Pulling a gold pocket watch from his vest, he pressed the latch to open the cover and observed the hands. "Perfect. One-thirty-six am. Take off ten for the buffer and round to one-twenty for departure time."

He would have twenty-four hours at that time point before the bubble forced him into the next jump. He could do anything he wanted between then, but it was imperative that he be back inside the house for the next one. If he missed it, the structure would leap forward without him, and he would have to spend a year in the past the long way, waiting to catch up.

His eyes adjusted to the dark of the room, he glanced around the small cottage in which he stood. A simple thing, all that remained of it in 2084 was a single cornerstone which had marked the location, and it had taken him three weeks to locate it. However, with a little extra planning, the building had been prepared and placed prior to his arrival and would remain intact for one day a year while the bubble held it in place. Stocked with furniture and a few supplies, he should be relatively comfortable during his stay there.

He had been doing this long enough that he knew exactly how to set up an outpost. This blind was perfect, and from the outside, no one would be able to tell it was a replica, and even from the inside, they would have to know what to look for if they hunted for flaws. "Damn, I'm good," he boasted to the empty room.

Dropping his leather-bound journal on the small table that stood in front of the large window, he pivoted slowly to examine the room. Behind him, the entrance to the cottage held precedence in the small foyer, and the sitting room he occupied lay to the left of it as you entered.

On the far back wall of the room stood a shallow fireplace, and a single sofa sat along the right-hand side. His large wardrobe trunk had been packed with a variety of attire and held the corner between the two, in front of a book case. The shelves were filled with period-correct knick-knacks, which spilled across the mantle as well. The chill in the air necessitated the fire, and he removed his coat and hung it over the back of one of the chairs to keep it fresh while he warmed the room.

Grinning at his pile of wood, he arranged a few pieces and a bit of kindling, then used one of the matches from a new box on the mantle to ignite the blaze. "Damn cold in here," he muttered, rubbing his hands together briskly, then offering them to the flames.

I hadn't anticipated the severity of the weather. But at least he had thought to pack a bit of wood, which he could always add to along the way using the axe stored in the kitchen. The thought of the extra time it would require stealing a bit of his joy, he breathed deeply, hoping to hold as much as he could. After a few minutes of repeating the rubbing and warming, he used the matches to light a candlestick from the table and explored the rest of the dwelling.

Across the narrow entrance, a second small room served as the kitchen, where another table could be used to prepare or eat meals. The fireplace in this room wider and deeper, it held a black pot dangling over the center of it. A large vat of water had been added, but he would have to use it sparingly if it was to last him.

Blinking at it a few times, he realized how long thirty-eight days would seem if he had to handle all of the workload himself. But he had made this jump alone, and he was on his own until the time bubble collapsed and sent him home.

He had been overjoyed at the journey's approval, but standing in the midst of it, his happiness was being sapped, overshadowed by apprehension. Flicking his gaze around the kitchen one last time, he returned to the foyer to make his way to the bedrooms in the back. Two in total, the doors to each were at the end of a narrow hall, facing one another with a small cupboard in the wall between, which lay parallel to and facing the front door of the cottage.

Behind it, a third fireplace could be accessed from either of the bed chambers, as it also occupied their shared wall and would warm the pair evenly if he chose to sleep in one of them. They appeared to have made the journey intact as well, but warming them would require even more energy and time; time he didn't have to spare. "It's fucking freezing in here," he grumbled, his dark mood pulling him further into his funk.

Small in size, each of the quarters held square beds that would seem quite cramped compared to what he was accustomed to. Normally, he wouldn't mind the conditions of the places he visited, but this one had put him on edge almost as soon as he had materialized. Holding up his candle, he inspected each of the rooms, then removed a blanket and heavy down-filled pillow from one of the beds. Closing both of the doors to the smaller chambers, he carried the bedding back out to the sitting room.

Longing to put the dark mood aside, he placed the candle on the table beside the window and removed his authentic boots. Propping them up next to the chair that held his jacket, he stretched out on the couch to sleep in the warmed air of the parlor. *It will work out,* he soothed to himself. *It can't all be perfect.*

When he awoke, the sun had risen, and he could hear the sounds of the fading embers sizzling inside the hearth. Pushing himself up, he rubbed his face with his hands a few times, still muttering about the cold before he stood to stoke the fire and add a few more logs. Watching the flames as they danced, he thought about the reason he had come to that place, and his pulse slowed with the realization he had made it, and soon enough his latest adventure would begin.

Feeling more relaxed, Nathaniel retrieved a basin of water from the vat in the kitchen and washed his face and had his shave. Then he lit the fire in the larger fireplace and prepared a small meal from the provisions he had brought with him. The special refrigerated crate that held his food was one of the few items he had brought that were not authentic to the era.

Analysts typically did everything they could to blend in and not risk being noticed while within a bubble. However, he had learned through the years that providing the bare necessities would allow for more time to explore and record while he was there, not to mention removing some of the risks of being made ill under certain conditions.

Besides, it's not like I'm going to bring anyone into the cottage, he mused. Savoring his eggs and sausage with rye toast, he thought about how his first Christmas Eve in the series would be spent. In his own time, he would have already been to the gym and had a shower, but some luxuries could not be packaged, and there was satisfaction to be had living as they had in the past.

Seated at the front window while he ate, he once again admired the view and thought of the young woman he had come to see. *I bet she's beautiful.* Or she would be, once she had grown up. *Currently, she's a newborn.* He chuckled to himself, the idea of it lifting his spirits as much as the nourishment.

Finished with his breakfast, Nate opened his field journal and penned a few lines.

Journal Entry

Arrival time and jump estimate is 1:20 am. A little earlier in the morning than I had hoped, but it will do. The cottage arrived safely, but the weather here is harsher than I had anticipated. I have sealed the back rooms and will make do with the kitchen and parlor. It's beautiful here, and I will leave shortly to try for the township on this first day. More to follow.

Once his routine had been noted, he unfolded the map he had prepared for the journey and estimated the amount of time it would take to hike to the township.

"Half an hour if I hustle." He grinned. "Not bad." Folding the parchment, he slid it inside his leather-bound book and secured it with the elastic band. Donning the heavy coat that would protect him from the winter outside, he dropped the journal into one of the large front pockets and prepared to get started on his short hike.

Nate felt over-dressed as he trotted down the steps and into the woods, but there had been enough analysts visit the area that he knew he would not be recognized as an outsider in his current attire. His attention to detail had earned him a great deal of prestige among his colleagues over the years, and he could go anywhere in time if he wanted, completely unnoticed by physical attributes when given the chance to prepare.

Normally, that fact would bring him a welling of pride within his chest, but not this day. As his heavy shoes clomped along the moist dirt of the forest floor, the melancholy he had been fighting as of late resurfaced. Typically, he would plan his itinerary, the jump would go smoothly, and he would return home to write his exposé.

After it was published, the accolades would begin, and he would enjoy a few months of mild fame before the limelight faded. His mouth pursed into a definite scowl, he recalled the loneliness of his existence. Once his latest story had become old news, none would hardly bother to acknowledge his presence, and so the hunt would begin again.

A new time period, a new target, a new exposé. The thrilling boost that would come with his success. "This is our drug now, theirs and mine," he deliberated as he left the wooded area to stroll down an actual path, the snow thicker outside the trees. Wide enough for a cart or carriage, two ruts had been worn into the soft earth, their indent in the white coating was unmistakable.

Using the right side, Nathaniel strutted along, his steps angry crunches as the sun shone upon him, providing little warmth with its golden shower. *Before the silent war, people wanted to be entertained,* he recalled. They wanted larger-than-life fiction, sometimes in the form of books but mostly as video. *Today, they want the truth.* That's why the department of historical research had been formed.

Using cutting edge technology, analysts such as himself made the jump into the past for their research, then provided those stories and adventures via their written exposés. Video and drama were a thing of the past, taken down and removed along with most of the things one might have known before the last great war. The conservation of energy and reduction in pollution were driving forces in the modern era, to be certain, and little of that gluttonous period remained.

Spying a cart on the road, he paused his step and his wallowing. Ambling towards him, and not in the direction he intended to go, he left the trail and crunched through the thick layer of snow a few feet away from the path. Glancing down, he knew right away it would be no use to hide within the trees. *Damn, I'm sure these tracks will lead right to me.*

Deciding to stand his ground and simply allow the carriage to roll past before he resumed his march towards town, he stood up straight and waited. To his dismay, the buggy failed to obey his silent command and stopped squarely beside him.

"You there!" A loud male voice shattered the quiet of the morning.

Flicking his eyes over, Nathan swallowed. His attire might pass inspection, but his speech would most likely not, especially since he had not prepared a back story that would stand up to any type of scrutiny. Blinking at the man hanging out of the door of the carriage, he improvised. "I beg your pardon?" he asked in the best accent he could muster.

"Are you daft, man? It's the dead of winter. What are you doing wandering upon the road without a horse or buggy?"

"I was… taking a walk," Nate offered, stepping towards the coach. "But I'm afraid I've lost my way. Is this the direction of town?" he asked, raising an arm to indicate the way they had come.

"Please, Alex, invite him in," a female inside the dark interior reproached.

Climbing out, Alexander Astrid held the door. "Right you are. Please sir, won't you join us?"

The slight bow of the gentleman strengthened his resolve, and Nathaniel climbed inside the cramped space. Taking an empty seat next to the window, he glanced out to see his tracks clearly in the snow. *Yup.*

Climbing in as well, Alexander reclaimed his place next to his wife. As soon as the cart began moving, the interrogation began. "Where is it you reside?"

"York," Nate lied evenly, his pulse calmed and his head clearer. "I'm staying with family for the holiday over at the old Rigby estate."

His eyes narrowed, Alex countered, "You mean new Rigby estate?"

"Yes, quite right," Nathan agreed quickly, his heart leaping again. "It was only finished last year, wasn't it." Mentally scrolling through what he had learned about the area in his pre-trip planning, he recalled that detail and a few others that might help him pull off his ruse. "I'm Nathaniel, one of the Rigby cousins."

"Ah, how quaint," Lenora spoke up, smiling at him as she cradled a bundle in her arms. "We are in for a holiday visit ourselves, here at the Astrid estate."

"Indeed, I am the son of Heloise and Aaron Astrid," the male of the group affirmed. "We can see you to the manor and perhaps you can be given a lift to your family's stead on the morrow."

"The morrow!" Nathan gasped. Recovering quickly, he added, "The morrow is Christmas."

"Yes, but it's at least twenty-five miles as the crow flies, and I'm afraid with this evening's festivities, it would be impossible to spare any of the servants tonight," Lenora explained casually. "Lady Astrid has plenty of vacant rooms, and there will be a fine dinner served. Surely you can enjoy a single evening in the company of new friends."

"What about this carriage?" Nathaniel pushed.

"In this snow, you would need fresh horses, in the least," Alexander advised, eyeing their guest curiously. "Come to think of it, you are a long way from home."

Seeing the doubt in his benefactor's eyes, Nate curled his tongue and fought the panic. "I'm sure I can stay for at least the dinner," he assured. "As for the ride home, we'll work something out. You are quite right. It was foolish of me to wander so far from the estate. My family will be worried for certain."

Glancing down at the bundle in her arms, then at the three boys on the seat next to him, a moment of clarity flickered within him, and he changed the subject smoothly. "You have a new baby," he fished.

"Yes, this is Gwendolyn," the mistress of the carriage beamed. "And these are our sons, Douglas, Adam, and Thomas," she informed him, indicating eldest to youngest with an open palm.

Grinning at his discovery, Nathaniel nodded. "How pleasant to meet you all. I will vastly enjoy your hospitality, rest assured."

The manor looming ahead, the carriage ambled in a wide circle and stopped when the door aligned with the large steps. Climbing out, the group was escorted inside, where Nate did his best to mingle unnoticed and gather all the information he could acquire.

Cottage Outpost
    December 25th, 1760 – year 1

Arriving at his cottage just after midnight, Nathaniel hurried inside, slamming the door in his haste. He had spent the evening in the company of the Astrids and had successfully made a quiet exit once the household of guests had begun to dissipate. Crossing the estate and entering the woods in the dark had been a challenge, but he had made it back with time to spare before the jump, hopefully leaving the curious Alexander none the wiser.

Dropping his journal on the table, he set about lighting the fire to warm the room, then prepared a pot of coffee over the fire in the kitchen. Having decided it would be easier to only heat the front half of the house, he brought out a second blanket and reclosed the door of the bedroom with a sigh.

His cup ready in a few minutes, he removed his coat and hung it over the back of the chair, then took a seat to drink the warm brew while he penned his first day's final entry.

Journal Entry - continued

With a bit of dumb luck, I was picked up by the Astrid family, or part of them, while making my way towards town. I spent the evening in their company, as they believe I am a member of the Rigby family, who own the adjacent estate.

At this point, I consider myself fortunate as these two families are not close friends and I am the first they have met or spent any real time with. In addition, I have been invited to return any time. An invitation I intend to avail myself of as soon as I have had a nap and arrive in the new year...

He added some further notes that would be useful when compiling his exposé. *This is after all a historical documentary,* he consoled, unable to completely hide his joy that he had found his target and had the perfect position established for watching her grow.

TWO

Christmas Angel

COTTAGE OUTPOST
December 24th, 1762 – year 3

Journal entry

Such an angel. I have never believed in such things, but even I must admit the possibility. Gwendolyn has reached her third Christmas, and a new Astrid was presented at the Christmas Eve Ball. Another boy, John, the family seems rather content with their single female and even more so with their string of males. I have returned each year as planned but have kept to the outskirts of the group as much as possible so that I may avoid Alexander's scrutiny. So far, they have either accepted my presence as perfectly natural or have overlooked me completely in the midst of their large and thriving family...

Nate's hand paused at that point, a jolt of sadness rippling through him. His fingers pressing against the page, the paper crumpled as he longed to scrunch it completely and rip it from the binding. "Overlooked me completely," he grumbled.

The truth was, most had done so his entire life. Besides a brief few minutes he had spent talking to Gwen, he felt certain no one inside the house had even noticed he was there.

Thinking of her beautiful features, he released his grip on the offending paragraph and drifted into the memory. She had been standing in a chair when he arrived so she could peer out at the falling snow. Her hair in long, golden ringlets, they framed her small face perfectly. Her dress immaculate, she didn't look like any child he had ever seen.

"What are you looking at?" Nate had asked as he casually joined her.

"Outside," Gwendolyn had sighed, the shake of her head causing her curls to glisten. "Tis a beautiful day for play."

"Hmm," he agreed, more or less. "But the snow would ruin your fine gown," he observed.

"As mummy says," she agreed.

She doesn't sound like a three-year-old, either, he silently observed. Pivoting to watch the room, the rest of the Astrid clan milled around, greeting one another, filling plates, and taking turns on the ballroom floor.

Returning his attention to the miniature woman next to him, Nathan coaxed, "Are you enjoying your holiday? Christmas is filled with magic, you know."

The girl had not replied and simply looked up at him with doleful mahogany orbs.

Shaking himself back to the present, he rebuked, "Get your mind back to the matter at hand. She's just a little girl, and by the time your trip is over, she'll be dead." His age by then but assuredly not among the living.

Continuing to stare at the page, a cold fear gripped his lungs, making it difficult to breathe. *She's the reason you came here.*

The idea tickled the back of his mind, and in all honesty, he had known since the first time he had seen her headstone that it had been true. Generally, he never missed his personal device on his trips, but tonight, he longed to hold it and to stare at the image that had inspired him. *Maybe then I could accept what fate awaits her.*

Cottage Outpost
　　December 24th, 1764 – year 5

Journal entry

. . .

Things have been better for me the last two years. I have made a conscious effort to refrain from speaking to any I do not have to, including Gwendolyn. She seems happier as well, but I suspect the family is less doting upon her because of her gender. The boys are all showered with praise and gifts, while Gwen stands alone in a corner or along a wall where she can stare out of the window year after year.

The war is brewing, bubbling in the background. Even the wealth of this family cannot protect them from what is coming, and I could feel the tension in their halls tonight, even as they gathered to make merry...

Cottage Outpost
December 24th, 1766 – year 7

Journal entry

There will be no more Astrid sons or daughters or at least not sharing the same mother. Lenora was lost in childbirth only a few weeks ago, and the family gathering seemed less jovial than in years past. Gwendolyn took the passing of her mother quite hard, and even my best attempts could not draw her away from her window or into the smallest of conversations...

Cottage Outpost
    December 24th, 1767 – year 8

Journal entry

If I had seen this in my preliminary research, I would certainly have dug deeper. The noble Lord Alexander has already remarried, a bride with three daughters of her own, no less. And judging from the bump under her dress, this brood will be housing a new edition before January is ended. On the bright side, Gwen appeared to be much happier and has taken to helping to care for her younger brothers in her mother's stead. Perhaps there is hope for her after all.

Cottage Outpost
    December 24th, 1769 – year 10

Journal Entry

The war continues to loom in the background, but the little mistress has definitely come into her own. Dressed in a fine gown, she handled herself beautifully. I don't recall seeing her at a window a single time all evening, as if she has suddenly noticed the world around her that is within her reach...

Blinking at the page, Nathan ran his hand roughly over his face. He had mingled as usual, over-hearing as much of the conversation in the room as he could, but in the end, it had been young Gwen who had stolen his attention and his affection. Her new stepsister Elenore was the same age, and the girls had the four next younger members of their hoard, two girls and two boys, well in hand while their mother tended to their latest addition. His target had never engaged in the expected behavior for her age, especially tonight as she had instructed them on proper etiquette at the ball.

Stealing only a few minutes to converse with her, something in her eyes had spooked him, and he pondered what his return to the ball might bring in the days and years to come. Replaying the memory, he hoped to ease the distrust and calm his fears.

"Your young siblings have a fine teacher," he had praised as she rebuked John in his slouched attire.

"It is my duty to preserve our family's func-tion," she replied tartly, not looking at him.

"And rightly so," he nodded, smiling down at the precocious girl who stood near chest high to him. Her hair darker than it had been, it still hung in tight ringlets that framed her flushed face. Her changes may have been subtle to her family, but seeing them one day to the next, a year of growth stood out boldly from his point of view.

"Do you attend our ball every year, Uncle Rigby?" she asked sharply.

"I have been invited to share the joyous occasion," he agreed. Steering the subject away from himself, he added, "I notice you no longer glare into the darkness beyond the panes, Miss Astrid."

"There is little use in longing for what lies outside, in the world of dreams," she sighed, returning her attention to the youngest of her four charges. "Merideth," she snapped. "One does not suck on their fingers in the midst of a family gathering."

Chuckling at her, Nate had longed to take her out and allow her to frolic in the snow he knew was falling outside. "Such a pity, to lose our ability to dream so young," he had sighed, mostly to himself at the moment.

Back in his cottage, he recalled the darkness of her mahogany orbs when she had turned them up to him. Something wasn't right with the young mistress of the manor, but he could not yet place his finger upon it. *Perhaps next year I will finally understand what has drawn me to her.*

THREE

Walk in the Woods

Forest Area
   December 24th, 1774 – year 15

"Gwen, we must go back," Elenore complained. Ahead of her, Gwendolyn Astrid, her stepsister born in the same year as she had been, tromped through the drifts of snow.

"A little longer," the taller girl with long honey-brown hair replied.

"But I'm freezing," the brunette insisted. "What are we looking for out here anyway?"

"You'd think I was mad if I told you," Gwen giggled, her voice hardly above a whisper.

"Well, stay with your search," Ellie grunted, turning on her heel and retracing her steps. "I'm going back to the house where a warm kettle awaits. The ball will begin this eve, and I intend to be ready."

Shaking her head, Gwendolyn let her go, strangely happy to have been abandoned. Turning through a bit of dried brush, the snow was not as heavy under the trees, as much of it had been gathered by the branches above. However, the ground stayed warmer as well, allowing a good deal of it to melt and form dark, gooey mud instead.

Outside his cottage, Nathaniel was using his axe to replenish his wood supplies when he heard the scream. The silence that followed heavy with anticipation, he listened intently. Lowering the blade gently to the ground, he turned slowly, the dilemma within him raging.

His primary goal above all others was to protect the cottage. Although it contained little that would incriminate him, it was his transport from year to year and eventually home. Keeping it a secret could prove the difference between making it back and being trapped in revolutionary America for the remainder of his life.

His breath frosting, he panted, the plain white shirt that he wore growing cold with the cessation of his movements. Damp with perspiration, it clung to his body as his chest heaved. Reaching for his jacket, he worked it on over the clingy material, his heart leaping when he heard the distinct sound of sobs.

"Well, crap," he muttered, running his fingers through his hair to tame the moist, mousy-brown waves. Following the muffled noises, he reasoned that offering aid would be more important than protecting his hideout, as leaving someone injured so near would only complicate his future jumps to subsequent years.

Pushing through the low-lying branches, he located the young woman as she lay in the mud. Her face hidden in her hunched state, she ran her hands over and gripped her ankle in turns as she cried.

Nathaniel knelt beside her, prepared to render aid but not ready for the moment their eyes met. "Gwen," he gasped, shocked to find her there.

"Hello," she breathed, forgetting her injury for the briefest of moments. "Uncle Rigby, isn't it?" she teased, then winced.

"Well, Nathaniel would suffice," he growled. "What the hell are you doing out here so far from the mansion?" He blurted the words, forgetting to hold to his customary attempt at an accent.

Her cheeks flushed, she knew in an instant her suspicions had been correct. "Looking for you," she leveled evenly. The man before her had aroused her curiosity when she was about ten, but it wasn't until after last Christmas that she had begun to put the pieces together.

"For me," he gasped, the wind knocked out of him for a moment. "Did someone send you?" Had someone noticed his annual visits? Being "made" was one of the main reasons such long trips were discouraged even if they were under the fifty-day limit on the use of their time bubble.

"No, silly," she giggled, grasping at his arm. "Please, help me stand."

Pulling her up, she leaned on the ankle, which promptly buckled.

"Fuck," he cursed as he caught her, earning him a dark glance.

"Such language," she whispered, her cheeks taking on an even deeper hue. "One would not expect to hear such a –"

"I know," he countered, cutting her off before scooping her into his arms. Able to support her easily, he grinned inwardly. *All those lonely trips to the gym have finally paid off.*

Taking his time so as not to lose his footing, he worked his way through the trees until he arrived at the cottage. Taking her straight inside, he closed the door with his foot, then carried her in to rest her upon the sofa he had been sleeping on.

Her eyes darting around the room, Gwen assessed the small space. The pile of blankets and pillow on the arm of the authentic furniture all fit well enough. *For a place that doesn't exist that is.* Holding her tongue, her heart raced as she waited to see what he would do about her crashing his secret residence, as he clearly had not come from the Rigby manor, if he ever had.

Busy preparing a soak for the injured appendage, Nate gathered a wrap from his emergency kit, squeezing it for a moment before deciding using it would be too risky. He would need to use traditional items if he were to have any hope of protecting his cover. Leaving it, he went to the back rooms and removed one of the sheets from the bed.

Back out front, he dropped it on the table and took his washing bowl outside to fill it with snow. When he returned, he removed her shoe and shoved her foot into the frigid slush. Looking up into her mahogany orbs as he knelt before her, he knew there would be no going back.

"Who are you?" she asked hoarsely, fear thickening her voice.

Sitting back on his rear, the man before her grunted, "I told you. I'm Nathaniel."

"And how did you do this?" she asked, indicating the house around them. "This building stands, but abandoned for years, not nearly so well. We played here in the summers before mother died. I know these ruins."

Her bottom lip quivering, he could see the turmoil within her, and rightly so. "You think I'm some kind of wizard." He chuckled, his mind instantly leaping to the few days he had spent researching witchcraft only a few years ago. "I guess it would appear so, from your point of view."

"What other sorcery could this be?"

Staring up at her, he held her gaze, searching for her trust. He was in a tough spot and damn well knew it. "Gwen, I wish that I could tell you, but I'm afraid that what I have to say wouldn't make any sense. Perhaps in time I can show you, but today, we need to focus on your injury. Tomorrow, perhaps –"

"You won't be here tomorrow," she clipped, cutting him off. "I've been watching, Nathaniel, trying to discern the truth." Wafting her hand at him, she stumbled over the words, searching for the combination that would explain her suspicions. "No one at the Rigby manor knows of you. I visited there last summer, and your name was not recognized by any of them."

Swallowing, he dared, "And what did your father say of this?"

"I did not speak of it to him," she spat, wiping at her tears while adjusting her numb foot in its cold bath. "I did not share my suspicions with anyone," she added, again meeting his gaze. "You're my special friend, Nate. The man who comes to me each Christmas Eve to share my ball. The man who magically never ages," she sighed.

"I see," he breathed, crossing his legs and running his hand roughly over his sparse beard he had not shaved yet. He would remove it before he dressed to leave for the Christmas Eve gathering, or at least he had planned to. His heart racing, he knew he needed to proceed with caution. "So, how do you think I have accomplished this friendship of ours?"

"I think you're a ghost," she confessed, raising her chin defiantly.

"A ghost," he coughed, his thoughts churning.

"I did," she agreed, cutting her eyes around the room again. "But I didn't realize spirits required sleep or a blanket to curl beneath," she theorized.

Grinning with pride, he couldn't help himself. "Good girl," he praised. "Excellent reasoning. I am not a poltergeist or a witch of any kind. I'm a man of science, but where I am from will be difficult to explain." Seeing a glimmer of light in the form of hope, he placed his hand upon her knee and leaned towards her. "Do you trust me, Gwen?"

"Of course I do," she whispered, another tear escaping to drip onto her cheek.

"Good. Then suffice it to say that I will explain everything to you when I am able, but it will be many years from now before I can. Let us strike a pact on the arrangement," he offered.

"What sort of arrangement?" she demanded a bit more forcefully, adjusting her foot once more.

Seeing that her snowy slush had all disappeared, he stood and began ripping the sheet into thin strips. "On your thirty-eighth Christmas Eve Ball, I promise to tell you how the cabin is made whole and how I came to be here. But you have to promise me you will tell no one of what you have discovered between now and then," he advised.

Watching him work with the thin material, she quickly calculated the time. "Thirty-eight, but that's over twenty years from now. You think I will wait that long to discover your secret?" she asked in a near shout.

Taking a knee, he lifted her chilled foot and dried it, then began applying the bandage. "Gwendolyn, you must trust me on this. I swear to you I will return every holiday and spend the eve with you, once a year, but that is all that I can offer. When we reach the l–" He halted abruptly, cutting off the word last and flicking his gaze up at her. Her large brown orbs glaring at him, he adjusted his tone, softening it as he continued, "When we reach the year of your thirty-eighth Christmas, I can share it all with you, but not before. And not if anyone else discovers the truth of my being here. If that happens, I'm afraid I will never be able to reveal it to you."

Holding the glare, Gwendolyn inhaled deeply, pushing the air out through her nose. She wanted to know it all, and she certainly didn't want to wait over a score to hear of it. "Are you certain this is the best accord we may strike?"

"Quite certain," he grinned. "If you can hold this secret, I will remain your special friend all the years that I can."

"Then we have a bargain," she agreed with a nod. Turning the foot, she examined the bandage that held it in place. "And how am I going to lace my shoe over this?"

"I doubt that you will," he confessed, grateful for the change in topic. "I'll have to carry you to the mansion, and there won't be any dancing for you this eve, I'm afraid."

"Have you no horse to ride me upon?" she asked in surprise.

"I'm afraid not." He grimaced, cleaning his mess and rolling up what remained of the butchered linens. "I'm here alone, and I walk everywhere I go. But don't worry. I'm as strong as an ox. I can carry you safely to the manor," he soothed with a wink in her direction.

Deciding they should have a bite to eat before they set out on the journey, he prepared one of the meals stored in his refrigerated crate, grateful it had been placed in the kitchen area and out of her curious view. While he warmed the meat and vegetables, he knew he was in trouble. *If she tells anyone about my being here, I'm sunk.*

However, trust was a two-way street. If she was to trust him, he would equally have to trust her. *Besides, this is the perfect time to gather the information for my expose,* he realized as he served their plates. Returning to the girl, he offered to help her into the stiff-backed chair.

"I can manage," she clipped. She set her jaw firmly, hobbling over and plunking down onto the hard surface. Looking over the meal before her, she noted the servings were only recognizable in the loosest sense.

"This is from my home," he explained, seeing the doubt on her delicate features. Taking the chair across from her, he cut at his meat and ate the bite with exaggerated chews.

Following suit, the girl tasted each in turn, then began to eat more eagerly at the pleasantness of the items.

Nodding at her willingness to accept what had been discovered so far, Nathan pushed, "Could I persuade you to answer a few questions?"

"What sort of questions?" she countered in surprise.

"Well, all sorts," he replied thoughtfully. "You could say I've come here to learn about you, or your people rather," he divulged, waving his fork to indicate the land beyond the walls of their small cottage. "I'm a scientist, as I said. I study things, like the people here, and I would love to hear about your life firsthand."

Reaching for her glass of water, she drank a few gulps, then sat up straight, recalling she was still a proper lady despite the strange man who shared her table. "I will answer what I am able," she replied, parroting his words with a half grin.

"Good." Opening his journal, he flipped to a blank page at the back of his entries and used his stubby pencil to take notes as she provided the intimate details that were always the hardest to gain.

Cottage Outpost
    December 24th, 1774 – year 15

Hours had passed, and the sun had all but set when he wrapped her in one of the blankets and lifted her into his arms. They set out through the woods, and true to his word, he carried her firmly tucked against his chest.

"You are stronger than you appear, kind sir," she teased. She had relaxed into his company a great deal in the time they had shared so intimately.

"I work out," he supplied, realizing instantly she would have no idea what such a thing could mean. Licking his lips, he focused on his balance as they reached the road, and his path would become easier.

When he felt safer in his steps, he explained, "Where I am from, people do things to improve their physical condition, such as walking or running. I like to also lift heavy objects to make my muscles larger and keep them firm." *Man, that sounds arrogant when you say it like that,* he realized inwardly with a short laugh.

Her hand resting on his chest as he held her, she had to agree his strength was evident. "Do all men participate in such activities?"

"A fair number," he agreed, working to hold his pace. Thinking of his modest home in 2084, he dared not tell her too much, as he had no real intention of telling her anything. The night she would wait for would never come, and when the final day of the bubble rolled around, he had no goal of visiting the manor or revealing anything to her even if she would lose her life the following day.

Manor House
　　December 24th, 1774 – year 15

· · ·

As Nate stumbled up the steps to the long porch that lined the front of her grandparents' house, Gwendolyn pointed out a chair with a tall back. "Put me down and let me sit."

"Why, we have to get you inside," he gasped, exhausted in his long hike with such a load. Not wishing her to see his pain, he swallowed, hoping he could at least manage a drink before he left.

"You don't want to be caught or questioned, do you? Unwrap my foot and take your blanket. I'll hobble inside and pretend it has taken me all this time to make it back. My stepsister knows I was in the woods. She can vouch for my story, and none will be the wiser," she predicted.

"Ah," he nodded, seeing that she had it all figured out. "So, you will hold to our bargain then?"

"Of course I will." She grinned, leaning towards him and planting an unexpected kiss upon his cheek. "Go, and I will look forward to our meeting next year, my ghost prince."

"Ghost prince," he hissed, prepared to argue the point if noises inside the house had not startled him more than the warmth of her moist lips upon his flesh.

Looking over her shoulder, Gwen stared at the door, expecting it to be flung open at any moment. "Please, Nate, all monkeyshines aside. Take your things and go before you are seen. I assure you I will be fine."

Quickly removing the wrap, his heart raced. When she stood and dropped the blanket into his arms, he curled it to his chest, covering the cold spot that had been left there when he set her down. "I'll see you in a year," he whispered, turning and trotting down the steps before he said or did anything else that might get him into trouble.

FOUR

Secrets to Keep

Forest Area
    December 24th, 1775 – year 15

Tromping through the woods, the blanket thrown over Nathaniel's shoulder reeked of her scent. *Damn.* The smell of her perfume made him giddy and made him feel guilty as hell at the same time.

"She's fifteen years old," he grunted aloud as he dove into the trees to hide his escape. Just as quickly, his inner self observed, "And tomorrow, she'll be sixteen. Give her a week, and she'll be old enough to date."

The idea of such a thing caused a sharp laugh to escape from him before he grew serious once more. *I wonder if she can keep my secret long enough for me to make it out of here.* More than twenty years from her point of view, a lot could happen in that length of time.

Arriving at his cottage a few minutes later, he closed the door behind him and leaned his back against it, as if holding out some evil force that had pursued him all the way from the mansion. His breathing slowed after a few minutes, he left the location and stoked the fire, ready to take to his sofa and get some sleep.

Kicking off his boots, he stretched out over the cushion she had occupied only a few hours before. *Gwen was here.* He had been obsessed with her for so long, and there she had sat before him while he tended to her wounded ankle. And tomorrow he would see her again, a year older and wiser, at the family's annual Christmas Eve Ball.

He knew the consequences of the evening's events could prove severe, and he considered hiding out for the remainder of the bubble, not leaving the safety of the cottage for the duration. *But if I do that, the trip will be wasted.* Glancing at the table, where his journal lay open to his notes on the day's conversations, he sighed.

"It would be enough," he commented aloud. She had been open and honest during her interview, sharing every detail he had asked for and then some. His hand lying on his chest, he patted it a few times with his fingers. "I can't do that to her. She trusted me with her story, and I can't simply disappear on her."

Rolling to face the back of the couch, he put the subject behind him. Closing his eyes, he would be asleep in a matter of minutes, and he would rise the following morning ready to face Christmas… again.

Manor House
    December 24th, 1774 – year 15

Watching as Nathan disappeared into the darkness, Gwen waited until she was certain he wouldn't be spotted should anyone come outside to look. Then, she forced her foot into her boot, leaving the laces dangling, and hobbled to the door of the mansion to let herself in. The pain unbearable, her face scrunched in agony as she half hopped over to the stairs a few feet from the entrance and sank down on the bottom step.

"Good heavens, where have you been!" her stepmother's shrill voice filled the air.

Producing genuine tears, the girl sobbed, "I fell in the woods. I should have come back with Ellie, but I didn't…" She trailed away, hoping Patience would draw the proper conclusions.

On cue, Elenore walked over to them. "Don't try to lay this burden upon me!" Her voice loud, several of the party guests stared in their direction.

"I do not blame you, sister. The burden is mine," Gwen countered, wiping at her tears. Trying to stand, she hoped to make it up the stairs to the sanctuary of the room that they shared before anyone else joined the questioning.

"You're really hurt," Ellie observed more quietly, climbing to stand beside her to the right on the third step. "What happened?" she demanded, honestly afraid the injury had been her fault.

"I told you. I fell in the mud almost as soon as you left me. I wish I had been as sensible," she coughed, leaning against the shorter girl.

Taking her on the left, Patience tested her forehead with the back of her hand. "You may have taken a fever. We need to get you into bed." Turning to the floor below, she spotted her eldest stepson and called loudly, "Douglas, come and carry your sister up to her room. She's injured her foot, and we need to see to it right away."

Oh my God, Gwendolyn squealed to herself. If she interpreted their actions correctly, they were going to see to her needs as if her version of events had been accepted. Lifted by her brother, she noted how much more difficult the task was for him. *Perhaps he needs to explore the concept of working out,* she speculated, pleased her plan appeared a success.

Still unclear on exactly how such a concept would be handled, she grinned to herself. Talking to Nate had been a purely electrifying experience and well worth the bedrest the adventure would cost her.

Placing her on the floor next to her bed, Doug grunted, "You should be more careful. You're practically a grown woman, not a child to be off running through the woods."

"I know," Gwen agreed, suppressing her smirk while he rebuked her. "I'll stay close to the house from now on," she promised.

"Yes, you will," he agreed, turning his back to leave them to her mending.

"Oh, he was quite upset," she observed when the three women were alone.

"Yes, quite, and for good reason," her step-mother admonished. "Times are hard these days with the growing tension between the colonists and the soldiers. It would appear that a war is on the horizon, and a dreadful one at that."

"Mother, please. She doesn't need a political lecture while we see to her wounds," Elenore sneered while helping her stepsister out of her dress, observing the mud-covered garment with a shake of her head. "You missed a fine evening by the way. Father has taken to inviting suitors to the ball, but you weren't here to be presented," she rebuked. "I fear you will have a scolding from him as well, once you are able to hear it."

"Well, that's a relief. The last thing I wanted for Christmas was a gaggle of suitors," the girl clipped, resting back on her pillow and covering her undergarments with the blanket. Only her right ankle exposed, she waited for the verdict.

Left alone with her thoughts while the others gathered their supplies, she recalled the afternoon they had shared. When it came to suitors, she could only think of one she cared to pursue. Nate's questions quite innocent on the surface, she wondered if he might have taken a liking to her in a romantic sense of the word as well. *And I have to wait a bloody year to find out,* she groaned inwardly.

"You're looking rather plum for having taken such a drastic tumble," Ellie observed as she placed a basin of cool water on the table next to her. Wetting a small cloth and wringing the excess, she used the rag to soothe her roommate's cheeks and forehead in turns.

Her face flushed at her starry-eyed thoughts of her rescuer, Gwen giggled. "I'm just thinking about suitors," she covered with the half-truth. "I hardly think we are old enough for such things."

"We aren't yet, but by next year we will be. However, the ones downstairs were here for you, not me," Elenore sighed, taking a seat on the bed next to her.

"What do you mean?" Gwendolyn asked in surprise. "We are the same age. Surely you will be given a dowry the same as I."

Licking her lips, Ellie looked around to ensure they were alone. "I am not an Astrid, Gwen. As much as our father loves me, and I am certain that he does, I do not carry the name or the blood that flows within your veins. I am certain you will marry far better than I in the end."

Seeing the sadness in her eyes, Gwen forced herself to sit up, that she might wrap her sister in her arms. "Do not fear such things, love," she implored her. "You will marry well and will have a happy life, of that I am certain." Of all the sadness in her days, at least Gwendolyn had been given a sister to share such thoughts and dreams with, but she dared not give up the one she cherished most.

Resting back against the pillow, a thick silence settled over them as Ellie tended dutifully to her scratches and wounded foot. Watching her, Gwen thought again about the questions Nathaniel had asked. *He would want to know about this,* she surmised. Unfortunately, she would have to wait a year before she could tell him.

FIVE

Rendezvous

FAMILY COACH
December 24th, 1775 – year 16

Gwen could hardly sit still in the carriage as it bumped along the familiar road. Sitting on the seat closest to the window, the woods to the left of them began only a few yards from the path. However, hidden somewhere within the trees lay a secret to which only she was privy.

Wishing she could stop the carriage and leap out, she wanted desperately to bound through the trails and knock upon his door.

"What are you looking at?" Alexander demanded, interrupting her daydreams.

"I was just thinking about last year and my fall," she sighed, again only supplying half the truth. She had become adept at lying over the years, and no one ever really seemed interested in what she had to say. *No one but Nathaniel,* she supposed, hiding her grin and returning her focus to the forest.

"Mind you stay at the house this holiday, young lady," her father snapped. "There will be guests to greet to be certain."

"Yes, father," the girl agreed in a quiet tone. He had made it quite clear over the last few months that he fully intended to have her married off by the next ball if he could manage it, and this was likely to be her last as a free woman. *Free woman,* she snarled under her breath. *There is no such thing.*

A woman of rank seldom made her own choices, and as surely as she would like to explore the possibilities with Nathaniel, her father would most assuredly select the man she would wed. The idea of it saddened her, and she blinked back tears as the trees disappeared behind them and the manor loomed ahead.

Cottage Outpost
    December 24th, 1775 – year 16

Awakening with the sun, Nathan washed and stoked the fire. Having his breakfast, he rehearsed what he intended to say to the girl who had visited him the day before. *Or last year as the case may be.*

The difference in time had never really bothered him before, but now that someone so important was making the long way around, it seemed to matter a great deal. *Maybe she's forgotten me,* he mused as he lathered his face and prepared to shave.

The likelihood of such a turn of events being small, he could feel a rock in the pit of his gut. It grew in weight with each passing minute, and he felt certain he would pass out if he didn't find out how things had turned out after he left her, and soon.

Washing out a few articles of clothing and hanging them to dry in one of the bedrooms, he selected a coat and pants from his trunk he had not worn before and prepared to make his way to the mansion. The girl had recognized him, but if he were careful, perhaps no one else would, and he could continue his annual visits. He still had not made the journey into town, which was one of the things he needed to discuss with Gwen. *One of these days, I will need to make my trip in that direction instead of the mansion and gather what I can from there as well.*

Knowing his history, there had been some battles during the year he had circumvented, and the following July would be the signing of the Declaration of Independence. *Next year, I should go to town,* he added more emphatically.

Dressed and ready well ahead of time, Nathan paced around the cottage, waiting anxiously for the sun to begin to set. Once it had, he could march through the woods and arrive at the mansion after the party had been underway for a time. *Better to be safe if I can,* he mused as he sat in his chair and made notes in his journal while he waited, mostly about what he knew of the year's events and questions he would like to ask the girl when he saw her.

When the appointed time had arrived, he placed the leather-bound book in his pocket and left the cabin. Making his way through the woods, he noted that the snow had been a bit heavier that year. Taking care not to slip on the covered foliage, he arrived safely at the path, and nearly a half hour later he stomped up the steps to the mansion.

Not bothering to knock, he let himself in and disappearing into the crowd of party guests as he had many times before. Almost immediately, he could sense the difference in the gathering. In years past, this had been a family affair, with many distant relatives making their way there for the event.

This year, he didn't recognize over half of the faces that he saw. *I didn't come last year. Perhaps they have simply changed too drastically,* he hypothesized. Then he spotted Gwen, and the reason for the strangers became abundantly clear.

"Oh, no," he grunted to himself. The group of men teeming around her, he could feel the rock in his gut turn at the realization. *She's come of age.*

Her father would be looking for a suitor. Immediately, he knew who the winner would be. *Geoffrey Earnest Romano*. He had seen the name on the grave next to hers, but the realization of that fact had not fully sunken in until that moment.

Blinking back tears, Nate pushed his way through the crowd until he arrived at the door and stumbled out onto the porch. Seeing the chair where he had placed her the year before, he extended his fingers and caressed the back of it fondly. *She will never be mine.* He had not fully accepted that fact, not for a moment. Not until he could see the swarm of men gathered around her, each of them hoping to have her hand. But he knew who would win.

Dropping his head back, he stared at the low covering of the roof above him, then ambled to the edge to lean against the rail.

"What are you doing out here?" a female voice caught him off guard.

Quickly wiping at his face to gather himself, he glanced behind him to see that it was Gwen. "Oh, thank God," he muttered. "You scared me. For a moment, I thought I would have to explain myself to the woman of the house."

"My grandmother is not well," she sighed, joining him in the cool air.

"Where is your coat or wrap?" he demanded, noting her already pale and prickled flesh. Removing his own, he dropped it across her shoulders.

"If I brought it, they would have followed."

She laughed, glancing at the door to ensure they were still alone. Flicking her gaze up to him, she could see the concern in his beautiful hazel eyes. "You worry for me," she observed quietly.

"Very much," he agreed, wiping at his nose. "I'm afraid I won't be able to make it next year. There are things I will need to attend to in town while I am here."

"That will be fine," she sighed, pulling his coat around her more snugly. "If my father has his way, I will be a married woman by then."

"Surely not," Nathan gasped. "Another year or two... or even three... might be in order."

"I'm afraid my time is up, Nathaniel dear," she taunted. Shifting her gaze to meet his, she whispered, "I've thought a great deal about us over the last year."

"Us?" he asked, his Adam's apple bobbing as he swallowed. "There isn't really an us, Gwendolyn."

"No, and I suppose there never could be. But that doesn't stop a girl from dreaming," she grinned, stepping towards him. "I always thought it was the magic of Christmas Eve that brought you to me. Do you not believe it could be so?"

Only inches between them, he stared down at her, considering how she might taste if he were to try for a kiss. *She's only sixteen,* his conscience screamed. *And ready to be married,* his other half pushed. Deciding to let her make the call, he waited, ignoring her reference to the supernatural the best he could.

Looking up at him, Gwen could sense the turmoil within him. "I have so many questions. I wish that I could have another day with you, alone, like we shared last year."

"I don't think that would be a good idea," he countered, not willing to back away from her. The scent of her perfume reaching his nostrils, he closed his eyes and sighed. "I really shouldn't stay long. The more time I spend here, the greater my chance of being noticed."

"Let me walk with you, then," she offered, darting around him and quietly descending the steps.

"Are you crazy?" he spat, catching her a few feet from the porch. "You're wearing my coat for one thing, and you would be missed for another, especially now," he added, indicating the house full of suitors with a wave of his hand. Seeing the hurt in her eyes, he stammered, "Gwen, I can't do this. I can't come back here again. I wish that I could, but there's too much at stake. My whole life, and maybe even yours."

"What about next year? You promised me a rendezvous every year," she whined, her features drawn as if she might cry.

"If you can make it into the woods early in the day, I could see you for an hour or two, but that's all that I can afford," he clipped, holding out his hand for his coat.

"I'll try to arrange it," she grinned, slipping off the jacket and placing it in his hand. Leaping to her toes, she used her free left hand to pull him down and pressed her lips to his. Not meeting resistance, she held the kiss, opening herself to him as the seconds ticked by and he reluctantly broke the connection. "I'll be thinking of you," she promised before pulling herself away and darting for the stairs.

Watching her go, she never looked back, and he wondered if she had any idea what would be in store for her during her short life. Wiping at his lips, he felt in a daze. Throwing the coat on, he turned away and began the long trek back to the cottage, his mind racing every step of the way.

When he reached the stoop, he let himself in and went through the routine of stoking the fire and preparing for bed. Once everything was in order, he reached into the pocket of his jacket as it hung over the back of the chair. The pocket empty, he thrashed about, feeling the material roughly and searching the rest.

Maybe I didn't take it.

Searching the table there by the window, then getting on his knees in front of the couch where his blankets still lay in a heap, he breathed in loud pants. *Nothing.* Getting to his feet, he stomped to the kitchen and had a look there. *Still nothing.*

"Oh God. She took it," he gasped. Darting back to the chair, he searched the coat again. *Son of a bitch!*

Pulling out his pocket watch, he glared at the face of it. *Twelve-thirty.* If he chanced it, the timing would be close. *Too close.*

Panic stealing his breath, he knew he really

only had one choice. He would wait for the bubble to push him to the next year and hope she brought it with her when she kept their date. *If she keeps it*, he grumbled, running a hand roughly through his hair. At that moment, all he wanted was to go home.

SIX

Betrothed

COTTAGE OUTPOST
  December 24th, 1776 – year 17

The following morning, Nathaniel stood at the window, coffee cup in hand. Watching the sun rise, he waited for her to show, aware that it might be hours before she did so, if ever. He hated to think what might have happened over the year his journal had been in her possession, and the repercussions could be disastrous.

Pulling the gold watch from his pocket, he glared at it, noting the time read a few minutes after eight. The sun low in the sky, it seemed like any other day. Squeezing the device firmly, he debated with himself, as usual. "Anything that happens is my fault," he cursed. He couldn't blame her, after all. He's the one who had put things in motion, letting his imagination get the better of him.

Once he had been a good analyst. *A careful analyst.* He didn't make mistakes, but that was before he met Gwen. Even at three years old, she had stolen his heart, and he had simply been waiting for her to be old enough, but to get there seemed impossible. The situation was a conundrum to which he held no solution. Even as his heart desired it, he knew the young woman would soon be betrothed to Lord Romano, and that would be the end of that.

Taking a large gulp of the liquid, he grimaced. "Damn... coffee's cold." Taking another drink, he longed for his microwave and his apartment and to be back in the modern world for more reasons than he could count.

Catching movement in the trees, he slammed down the cup and bolted outside. The freezing air smacked him in the face and stole a bit of his rage as he jogged across the yard to meet her when she cleared the trees.

"Good morning," she sang with a grin, flinging herself into his arms and giving him a firm hug. "My, you're chilled. You'll catch a cold —"

"Where is it?" he demanded, cutting her off.

Pulling the brown leather book from beneath her coat, she presented it to him. "No one saw. I promise," she soothed, holding her tantalizing smile.

Accepting the offering, he studied the cover,

caressing it gently. Then he flipped the pages quickly before glancing around. "You weren't followed?"

"No. We arrived last night, and everyone is busy with the plans for the ball today," she explained, pushing past him and making her way inside. She should have told him then the reasons why, but in that moment, she only wanted to share the comfort of his company and pretend the rest away. *As I have always pretended the rest away,* she confessed to herself.

"So, I take it your new husband doesn't keep such close tabs on you," he replied tartly, his words a dig he could not suppress.

"We have not wed yet," she sighed. "Tonight, my father will announce our engagement."

Looking up, he caught a glimpse of the sadness on her features before she forced it away. "You are not in love with your intended," he observed, the suffering clear in her mahogany orbs.

"My father chose my future husband to suit his own purposes. What they are, I cannot say, but my fiancé's are quite clear. Geoffrey Romano is twenty years my senior. I will be his third wife and likely his last attempt to have a son," she informed him quietly. "I am certain he holds as much regard for me as I hold for him."

Her eyes fixed on his, they stared into each other's souls. The house so quiet he could hear the tick of the watch in his pocket, Nathaniel pursed his lips, then changed the subject. "Thank you for returning it," he said calmly, holding the journal up to add weight to his words.

"I wrote in it," she replied, a small grin on her lips. "You are a time traveler. That's why you are only here one day a year. You could have said," she finished with a giggle.

"I didn't think you would understand," he replied crisply, turning his back as he flipped the pages to find her words. When he came to the questions he had written, hoping for the chance to ask them, he discovered she had responded to each and every one and then some. Running his fingers lightly over her fine hand, he added, "Thank you. This will be most helpful when I make my next report."

"Is that why you do it?" she asked, inspecting his quarters more closely now that she knew the truth about its existence.

"To learn about the past, yes," he agreed with a firm nod. Realizing she had read every entry, she had learned of the missions he had taken for the last eight years. Raising the gaze to her, he studied her profile, as she had become quite engrossed in something on the mantle. "You look older," he observed aloud.

"I am older," she agreed. "For each night you spend in this room, I age a year. What happens to me on the last day of your visit?"

"What?" he stammered, unsure why she would ask such a thing.

"You are very specific in your notes. I was born the year you came here, and you intend to leave the year I am thirty-eight. The year you promised to tell me everything. I assume that is the year that will be your last, so my question is why. What's so special about that Christmas Eve over any other?" Her eyes flicking around her, she pushed, "Does it have anything to do with the war?"

"What about the war?" he grunted, his mind racing as he desperately hoped he could avoid the truth at all costs.

"We declared our independence from Britain this year," she explained with a shrug. "The fight will not stop until we have won our freedom or they have forced the will to have it out of us."

"Oh, Gwen," he sighed, seeing the depths of her concern on her delicate features. Closing the book, he placed it on the mantle and pulled her into his arms, rocking her gently side to side. "I wish that I could tell you, but I'm afraid it would do more harm than good."

Clinging to him, she sobbed, "I know, and I don't really want you to tell me. After reading your journal, I realized how important this work is to you. And how dangerous it could be."

"Exactly," he agreed, inhaling her scent as he squeezed her. "I'm going to go into town from now on and leave your family alone."

"Can I still come and visit you?" she asked quietly, half afraid that he would deny her and the other half afraid that he would say yes. How easy it would be to remain there with him and leave her life behind.

"I'm not sure that's a good idea," he sniffed, fighting his tears. *How the hell did I become so attached to her?* The question hanging in his thoughts, he waited for her protest, but it did not come. "Why would you want to come back here?" he tried a different route.

"Well, truth be known, I've grown quite fond of you, Nathaniel Crabtree," she informed him tartly as she stepped out of his embrace, pushing him away.

"How?" he faltered, then started again. "I'm fairly certain I never spoke my full name."

"It's in the front of your journal," she teased, pleased she had gotten the better of him, for the moment at least. "You don't have to tell me anything about your life or where you come from," she offered, swallowing her sadness. Her voice quavered as she added, "And I know this whole age situation is awkward for you."

"Damn. I shouldn't have written all that," he observed.

"No, it's quite all right," she countered, toying with a small figurine in the shape of an angel. "It clarified my understanding. And when I return next year, I will be a married woman, so we can put all romantic notions behind us."

"Then why come?" he asked again, confused by her choice.

"Because you are storyteller, are you not?"

"Well, yes, in a manner of speaking." Her words setting off alarm bells, he recalled that was exactly what he had told Paul Hidalgo before his venture had been approved; Gwendolyn Romano would be the edge he needed to make this next exposé the most incredible of his career. "You want me to tell your story?"

"Yes, Nate," she grinned, her face damp with tears. "My life is not extraordinary, but it's all that I have. The idea that others might hear of it, study it, and even learn from it makes all the sadness seem somehow... worthwhile."

"Are you that unhappy?" he asked, not sure he really wanted to know.

"I'm going to marry a man twice my age for the sole purpose of giving him a son," she replied with a shake of her head. Raising her hand, she toyed with the curl that hung in the center of his forehead. "At least this way I can go home and pretend to myself that I could have had a different one."

SEVEN

Imperfect World

COTTAGE OUTPOST
December 24th, 1777 – year 18

Lying in the darkness, Nathaniel had hardly slept through the night. He had gone into town, as he intended, but nothing there held his interest. Oh sure, there was lots going on, but none of it seemed to matter knowing Gwen was being presented to her family as the future Mrs. Geoffrey Romano. *As if she were a side of beef offered up for a barbeque.*

They had shared the day before that, drinking coffee and talking about her life. Hearing her describe the events he had witnessed and the ones in between, he could not deny how deeply he cared for her. With the regal way that she carried herself, her blood lines were obvious to the trained eye. *She'll make him a fine wife, whether he deserves one or not.*

Shaking off the angry thoughts, Nate rolled off the couch and began to prepare for her return, if she were able. While he dozed, or attempted to, she had taken the other man's name and lived another year of her short life. He wanted to think ill of Lord Romano, needed to really, but he actually knew very little about the man that Gwendolyn had married.

"I'll guess I'll find out today when she gets here," he grumbled as he set the kettle to make his morning brew. "Adding him to the exposé would only be natural."

Reading through his notes over breakfast, Nathan could feel the familiar ache in his gut. It had almost been a constant companion since he arrived there and seeing her description of life as a woman of rank in revolutionary era America, he understood why. *This place is barbaric.* But he wasn't here to change the past; he merely needed to record it. *I'll have to keep that in mind while she's here today.*

Closing the book as the sun rose, he stared at the tree line. When the sun was higher in the sky than he would have liked, he began to pace the small room. Nathaniel wanted desperately to hold his enthusiasm for this particular assignment, but it had grown more difficult as he moved from year to year. He had known before he got there that her life had probably been difficult. Seeing it unfold had only added conviction to that notion.

People don't die at the age of thirty-eight because they had an easy life, he pondered with a wry grin.

No, it was to see the sadness in her eyes and her days first hand that troubled him deeply. He wasn't sure what he had expected to find, but this certainly wasn't it. *I only hope I can do this story justice when I'm finally able to tell it,* he sighed.

At that moment, a slender young woman sauntered out of the woods. Over her arm, she carried a basket, her coat and hair pristine despite the woods she had come through to get there.

"Shit," he muttered, her appearance terrifying. Meeting her at the door, he growled, "Why are you dressed like that?"

"I am expected to dress like this," she assured as she entered, glancing around before she sat their meal on the table. "I brought lunch," she informed him, indicating her load.

"I saw," he grunted. "You don't think anyone would find it odd you brought a picnic in the dead of winter?"

"Actually, I don't really care," she replied with a twisted grin. "I have but one day a year to spend with you, and with the war gaining in strength, I fear I won't see that thirty-eighth Christmas that you promised."

"Oh, you'll see it," he replied with a shake of his head, "provided you don't do anything foolish and get us both caught." He had never been in a situation where history might have been altered and wondered if he would know if or when it had been.

Opening the basket, she removed a plate of cheese and bread, followed by a bottle of wine. Placing them on the table, she began to rummage through the rest.

"You're mad," he chirped, snatching up the libation to inspect the label.

Cutting her cool brown eyes up at him, she swallowed visibly, then replied in a quiet voice, "I have but one day with you, Nathaniel. Please, allow me this one fantasy. Do not smash it so willingly."

Meeting her gaze, he could feel the sadness radiating from her. "Is it that bad?" he asked more gently.

"Find us some glasses, and I'll tell you all that I can," she agreed, forcing a smile she didn't yet feel, but she intended to. When he had turned to the kitchen to do as she had asked, she called after him, "I've been thinking about our situation."

"Of course you have," he agreed, returning with a pair of small cups. "I think these will do," he offered, opening the bottle and pouring for both of them. "What have you concluded about our situation."

"I think this one day exists outside of real time," she explained. "As if it was stolen and belongs to the two of us alone. Call it Christmas magic, if you will. Although, I fear you see no truth in such things."

"You seem to be obsessed with that notion, as

if this day were different from any other," he sighed. "If you are implying there are no consequences for what we do, my dear you are mistaken," he countered, raising his cup as a toast before tasting the rich flavor. "This is good," he said in surprise, then helped himself to a few bites of the cheese.

"My husband makes it. He owns a vineyard, which I contemplate is the cause of his drive for an heir, and the reason my father has chosen to bring him into our family. Alexander has six natural sons, and yet he seems to dote upon the one whom he chose for me to marry."

"I see."

"You do see." She smiled genuinely. "You always have, and I believe it is the force that has drawn me to you." Taking her cup, she sat in her chair to face him and provide details for the past year. "Since you are sacrificing your time here with me, I brought you some other things you might find of interest." Pulling out a sheaf of papers, she laid them upon the table between them.

"Oh my," he gasped, fingering them gently. "These are rare."

"Not to me, but in the future, perhaps. Will you be allowed to take them with you?"

"Yes. Everything in the house will go with me when the bubble collapses," he explained. "I may keep them private though. My own personal collection." His cheeks flushed, his pleasure at the offering apparent.

"Do you not normally collect memorials for your journeys?" she asked in surprise.

"No. Not like this," he allowed, examining a folded page more closely. "Oh, Gwen," he breathed. There could not have been a more perfect gift. "Thank you. I will cherish these always."

Her lips twitched as she held her smile. "Do you have questions for me today?"

"I always have questions. Tell me about your wedding. Did you feel like a princess?"

Her lips curling genuinely, the woman across from him dove into her tale, sharing the weeks leading up to her nuptial and every detail she could recall about the big day. "It's been a very ordinary year," she added when she had finished. "Geoff works endless hours with his wine making, and I am often left to my own devices. I have not conceived as of yet, but I'm sure it will happen soon, and I will have fulfilled my purpose in his life."

"If you bear him a son," Nate added, his words sounding a bit callous even to his own ears. "Sorry. I didn't mean any offense with that observation."

"None taken," she replied, sipping from her cup. "I have resigned myself to the truth of my existence." Running her tongue over her lips to wet them, she wished they had taken the couch instead. Standing, she walked around the room aimlessly, hoping he would join her.

Picking up on the vibe, Nate ran his fingers

through his hair as he considered addressing the elephant in the room. Deciding he could avoid it if he simply stayed put, he continued with his queries until the afternoon was spent and she gathered her things to leave.

"Are you certain you will not come to the ball?" she asked quietly as she packed the last of her things to leave.

"Quite certain. I'm going to look through your offerings and get a good night's sleep," he replied stiffly.

"You did not rest well?" she observed, looking up at him with wide mahogany orbs.

Resisting the urge to touch her, he kept his form stiff as he glanced at the door. "No. I've had a lot on my mind," he confessed. "But today was a beautiful day, Gwendolyn, despite the chill in the air. Perhaps I will rest well this eve and you will find me better company on the morrow."

"On the morrow," she echoed, her features losing their warm glow. "Another year," she whispered more quietly.

"Have a good one, Gwen," he offered, walking past her and opening the door to show her out.

"I'll come as early as I can," she agreed, leaving in a rush to hide her tears as she stumbled through the dusk in the forest alone.

EIGHT

In the Shadows

Forest Area
    December 24th, 1787 – year 28

Making the trek down the familiar path before the light had even begun in the east, Gwendolyn's mind turned each of her previous visits for inspection. Each year she came and shared the day with this strange man. Christmas Eve, she truly believed it was a magical time despite his refusal to see it, and even more so to her for this reason. He was indeed a strange man but not a stranger to her.

Each time she made the journey to his cottage, she held the hope that he would become her lover in the truest sense of the word, and each time she left hoping her disappointment did not show. He was a gentleman if ever there was one, and she had decided if they were ever to consummate their relationship, she would be the force behind it.

Ten years had passed since the summer she had married Geoffrey, and over the years, her life had been a stream of discontent. This year, near the end of October, she had given birth to her third child. This one had been a son but stillborn as the two girls before him had been, and it had left her wondering if she or her husband were being punished somehow. Her lip trembling, she cried, hoping to clear her sadness before she arrived at the line of trees ahead of her.

Wiping the drops of sadness away as she entered the woods, she forced her thoughts to more pleasant things. Her dreams taking hold, she focused on Nathaniel and the loving way he had always regarded her. Imagining herself naked in his small room, the light of his fire bathing her supple skin, she knew this year she would not take no for an answer. She needed him, and her time to have him ebbed with each day they had to share. *Soon there will be none, and I must not lose another chance.*

Arriving at the cottage earlier than she had in years past, the sun had barely cracked the sky when she opened the door and let herself in. Glancing to the left, the couch lay empty, as did the kitchen to the right. However, that room held the kettle over the fire, and the scent of his coffee filled the air. Dropping her wrap over one of the chairs, she noted his special crate that held his food and smiled at the ingenuity of the future. "If only I could see it," she observed, running her fingers over the top fondly before the door opened and Nate leapt inside.

"Oh, man that's cold," he talked to himself, not realizing she had arrived. Instead of addressing her, he stomped the mud off his boots and then removed them, dropping them beside his chair. Blowing warm puffs of air into his hands, he turned to help himself to his morning brew when he came face to face with her.

"Shit," he sputtered. "What are you doing here?" Wiping at the shadow of hair on his chin, he could only imagine the picture he presented.

Grinning at his rugged good looks and stubble-covered cheeks, she replied tartly, "I have a standing invitation." Taken with the idea of getting straight to what she had come for, she sauntered past him. Selecting one of his blankets from the sofa, she spread it flat upon the floor in front of his fire.

"What are you doing?" he gasped, frozen in place.

Her grin unshakable, she glanced at him, then began unbuttoning her dress.

"Hey, don't do that," he practically shouted, stepping forward to prevent her from unclasping any more of the tiny devices.

Dodging him playfully, she laughed, then taunted, "You silly man. Did you really believe I would come here all these years without demands of my own?"

Holding his position, he watched as the

elegant gown was tossed over the arm of the couch. The undergarments of the age less provocative than those in the future, he still had a chance, but a slim one. "What exactly is it that you're demanding?" Swallowing, he added, "You know I can't become involved in this time line."

"You were involved the moment you arrived here," she countered smoothly, removing her shoes and stockings and dropping them beside the fire.

"Gwen, I —"

"Don't," she closed the distance between them and pressed her hand over his mouth. "Ten years I have waited for you to place your hands upon me."

"I would never," he stammered from behind her palm.

"I know you wouldn't, but now you don't have to," she whispered, running her free hand up his chest and pulling at his shirt to remove it. "I want this, Nathan. I need it so desperately. You cannot fathom how far I will go to make you mine."

"But you are married to another man," he insisted, catching her hands and holding them to prevent any further action on her part.

"I belong to him, Nate. There is no love between us," she insisted.

"But there is a vow, and I do not wish to break it, or for you to do so," he stated hoarsely, aware he had already broken it within his heart.

"Does a promise forced by my father and the

expectation of my family hold me to blame? It is unjust to think that it should," she replied, her voice cracking. "Damn," she cursed, having hoped to avoid the tears. The years had shown the truth between her father and Geoffrey's motives, and her wellbeing had never been among them.

Seeing her distress, he grinned crookedly. "I've never heard you swear before. Not in all the stories and heartache you have shared."

"I've hidden the deepest pain well," she challenged, wiping at her damp cheeks.

Catching her chin, he lifted it to peer into her eyes. "You are so special to me, Gwen. You cannot imagine the guilt I have endured as a result of it."

"Oh, I can imagine quite a bit, of both guilt and endurance, my love," she sniffed. Seeing his moment of weakness, she raised her mouth to his, her lips searching for his submission. Her fingers working their way up his chest, they plunged into the back of his hair and toyed with the nape of his neck.

"Gwendolyn," he breathed, breaking their connection but not removing himself from her grasp.

"Nathaniel," she replied in a husky tone, pulling at him to press his body against hers. "Never have I held a man of my own desire or felt the joy in the joining of our bodies. Please, do not deny me this."

Pivoting, as if to tear himself away, Nate's eyes landed on his journal. The plain leather cover closed, he knew the words hidden within. Her words, as she had bared her soul to him, sharing every intimate detail of her life. Inhaling the scent of her, it called to him, enticing him to give up on the questions and prodding, at least for this one day. Placing his hands on her hips, he traced the line of her, admiring the feel of her cotton undergarments.

"You know, I find these vintage outfits sexy as hell," he confessed.

She only giggled in reply, torn between kissing him and tearing his clothes away before he changed his mind.

Cottage Outpost
December 24th, 1787 – year 28

Lying on the blanket she had spread on the floor and covered with the other, their two naked forms intertwined as a Greek sculpture might. He could not deny he had enjoyed the taste of her, the exhilaration beyond any love he had ever made. *Or perhaps it's the fear of getting caught,* he justified to himself. They were, after all, in a cabin on her family's land, with her husband, father, and brothers all unlikely to approve of their current state.

"I can't believe I actually did this," he said

aloud, his fingers tracing her perfect curves playfully.

"Yes, it was certainly hard to convince you," she teased.

Pushing the blanket down, he admired the beauty of her breasts and skin, then paused when he reached a large green splotch that covered her ribs beneath the left. "I didn't do this, did I?" he gasped, thinking of his grip upon her when he had been lost in the throes of passion.

"No," she clipped, pulling the blanket back over the section of flesh, an obvious attempt to hide it. She didn't speak the words, and she didn't have to.

"How long has this been going on?" he demanded, sitting up straight and removing the cover with purpose. Holding her down, he ran his fingers over her, looking for other signs of abuse.

"Nathan, please," she begged, struggling to free herself. Finding her resistance futile in his firm grasp, she gave up and lay still while he completed his search.

"He beats you," he concluded, the evidence clear. "Your clothing hides that fact. Is that why you wanted to be my lover? To expose the truth in your relationship with him," he accused, getting to his feet and searching for clean clothes. She had never mentioned it before. Had she climbed into his bed as her way of admitting this ugly truth?

"No, of course not," she replied, pulling the blanket around her to cover herself while she located her own.

"Then why? Why now?"

"Why not now?" she countered. "It's been ten years since this really began, and I only have ten left to hold you," she asserted, her voice broken by the end. Her tears came in a hot rush, surprising them both.

"Gwen, I'm so sorry," he gasped, happy with his underwear for the moment. Catching her, he pulled her into his arms and wrapped her tightly.

"Do you know what it's like?" she sobbed. "To know when the end will come? It looms over me like a shadow. You will leave, and I will never see you again. You have been the only light in my life for so long. How will I go on without you?"

Brushing the hairs out of her face, he studied her, considering his words carefully. *Man, this was a big mistake.* And he wasn't just thinking of taking her to bed. Allowing their meetings, following her life, even coming there had been too much. *But it's too late now.* It was a slippery slope he had had no way to avoid once that first step had been taken.

"You'll manage," he said aloud, hoping he could keep his secret and she would never discover his true intent of coming there.

"Yes," she agreed with a loud sniff. "I will have ten days of passion to remember you by, if you will allow me them." She didn't blink at her choice of words, fully meaning them.

"I had not guessed you were so fiery inside that bodice," he teased, enjoying the feel of her in his arms. *This is so wrong.* He knew he could be fired for less, but he felt powerless to resist her charms.

"Then you will agree to my offer?" she grinned, hope welling within her.

"I will on a single condition," he acquiesced.

"Name it," she giggled, pulling away to continue her search for her clothing.

"I want you to have a long and happy life, Gwendolyn," he observed, as close as he had ever come to affecting the future. "Can you promise me that you will try?"

Pausing to fiddle with her stockings, she didn't face him until she had screwed her face into the proper proportions. "For you, I can do no other."

"Even after I'm gone," he pushed. "I want this so badly for you."

"And you shall have it," she agreed, nodding profusely. "I promise. I will do my best to live a long and maybe even happy life."

Shaking his head at her manipulation of his words, he grabbed her arm and pulled her to him. Giving her a squeeze, he laid his head against hers and breathed. *I really hope you can.*

NINE

Days to Years

COTTAGE OUTPOST
December 24th, 1792 – year 33

Gwen lay across the blanket they had spread over the floor, as had become their custom. She would arrive early and join him in his sleepy state, removing their clothing and making passionate love until midday. Once they were satiated, they would wash and dress to spend the afternoon talking over a light lunch. He loved that about her, the ease with which she could share his bed, his journal, and his life.

Leaning over, he blew gently across her ear. She hardly stirred, and he chuckled at her slumber. "Silly woman. Sleeping away our hours together." But he didn't mind, not a bit. Pushing the blanket down, he inspected her back, noting the old bruises and a few fresh ones. She had presented herself last year with a split in her lip, one of the few times Geoffrey had struck her in the face, or so she claimed.

Nate had no way of knowing, and it was probably a good thing. He suspected she hid the abuse she suffered from everyone, and it tormented him that he alone should know her secret. He still wasn't sure he would be able to talk about it in the exposé, but he knew the story would never be complete without it.

"What are you doing?" she interrupted his cerebral moment.

"Honestly, thinking of killing your husband," he jested.

"What?" she gasped, rolling and sitting up at the same time, pulling the blanket with her to cover her bare breasts.

"I'm only kidding." He laughed, holding up a hand to prevent her further dismay. "Men are still cavemen at heart, and it makes my blood boil to see what he's done to you."

"Cavemen?" Her voice quavered as she pushed her long honey-colored hair away from her face. "I don't understand the reference."

"Primitive. Wild. As advanced as we are in the future, we males tend to be a bit possessive of our women, and having someone hurt them is not allowed," he explained, toying with her golden locks as well.

It gave her heart a flutter to hear him say such things. "I wish that I could be yours," she admitted softly.

"I know you do, and in my heart, I feel the same. But we both know a few stolen days are all that we may share." He grimaced, the jagged thought of what their time would probably cost him when he got home gutting their moment.

"What troubles you?" she asked, using her fingers to smooth the lines in the face that never aged.

"We have five days left, after this one. Let's get dressed and have our lunch so we can chat while we still may," he suggested, avoiding the darkness that had brought his foul expression.

"Or we could hide beneath the covers and pretend the world away," she countered wistfully.

Her eyes crinkled when she giggled, and he could see the years wearing upon her. For each night he spent waiting for her, she endured a year of torment just to make it back to him. "I wish that we could," he confessed. "But it's better to complete a few more pages of research. That is the reason I came here after all."

Rolling over and getting to his feet, he missed the hurt expression that flittered across her delicate features. After all this time, he still could not confess the real reason he was there. Standing to join him, Gwen located her undergarments and added her clothing in layers.

"I'm surprised you don't have any children yet," he observed absently. "I know you lost the three, but it has been five years since the last one."

"I don't think I will conceive again," she mumbled, adjusting her corset.

"How'd you manage that?" he asked in surprise, pausing with his shirt draped over his hands as he faced her. "I wasn't aware that birth control existed so far into history."

"He doesn't touch me with anything but his fists these days," she replied, not meeting his gaze. "I know you have promised I will be here for our final hours, but I fear each time that he will kill me before that day can arrive."

"Oh my God. Now I really want to murder him," Nathaniel seethed.

Her hair floated briefly when she spun to face him. "You will do no such thing, Nathan Crabtree. I haven't spent all these years enduring his abuse and sharing my life with you to have you throw it all away in a moment of weakness."

"What's that supposed to mean?" he snapped, resuming his grooming and getting dressed.

"It means you have to go back to where you belong. You have to share what I have told you. All those pages we have filled cannot have been in vain." Her voice cracked, and she sniffed, her tears hiding behind her glorious waves.

"Aw, honey," he groaned. Catching her to remove the curtain of hair, he caressed her drops of sorrow away. "It will never have been so, I assure you. Please do not allow my words to give you pause. I will never raise a hand to your husband or divulge my existence to him or your family. I promise."

Nodding, her chest heaved spastically as she coughed, overcome with grief. Regaining her fortitude, she managed a weak smile. "Thank you. You are a good man, and I am grateful I have had the chance to know you."

Simply nodding, his face pasty white as he watched her, he indicated her chair. "I'll make us lunch, and you can tell me about your year," he offered.

"Well, that won't be pleasant," she quipped. "We lost grandfather in the fall."

"Aaron is gone?" he stipulated while searching the crate for their meal.

"Yes. He had been ill almost as long as I've been alive," she pointed out. "He hadn't been down the stairs in over a decade, maybe a score. As it were, he has been laid to rest in the graveyard."

"The one next to the old church?"

"Yes," she agreed with a giggle, noting his habit of referring to everything as old when in fact it wasn't at all; at least not to her.

Pausing, a moment of grief overwhelmed him before he pushed it aside. *I can't let on who else is buried there,* he inwardly battled, but the image of her gravestone hung in his memory. Using the pot to warm their meat and vegetables, he carried on. "Any good news from this year? How's the war going?" he asked, being polite, as he knew how it was going.

"I suppose it's going well, or what I hear of it," she sighed. "I hope we are near the end."

Cutting her eyes over at him, she surmised he was aware of when it would in fact end but didn't dare ask for the detail. Instead, she observed, "The soldiers on both sides were housed by the farms and estates around us, as well as on our own. We have been plundered. It will take years for us to recover, regardless of which side wins."

"I guess you already know who wins," he interjected, his tone bleak. "I'm sorry. I just this moment realized my notes probably gave it away and you've known all along."

"I suspected," she affirmed. "You referred to this time period as the American Revolution, and one can only assume it would have been given another name if the redcoats had managed to take us."

"You are such a smart lady," he praised.

"Smart enough to hear at last how you have constructed this cottage every year?"

"That's a secret for our last day," he teased.

"But you know I'm not going to tell anyone. And if you tell me now, I'll have time to consider it and ask you questions next year if I like," she insisted. "Do you not trust me?"

Leaning back in his chair, he glared at her, an idea in the back of his mind that should not have been. Curling his tongue, he allowed it to unfold so he could tuck it away and make sure no part of it tumbled out of his mouth. When he felt it had been secured, he began with what he would be able to divulge. "In the future, we have machines that are very useful."

"Like your crate of chilled food," she suggested.

"Yes, exactly like that but many times over and used for every part of our lives." He paused for a moment, thinking of how every part of his world under normal circumstances was shaped by the technology and advances that had been made between their two times. Life had been much simpler in her time, for certain, despite how she felt about it. "One of these machines is able to create the bubble in which the cottage exists," he concluded in a single sentence. He stood to gather their plates, as if that explanation alone should have sufficed her.

When he returned to the table, he found her staring at him expectantly.

"That doesn't tell me anything," she pointed out when he began to eat without another word.

"Well, the rest is a bit more complicated. First, you have to know what a planet is, stars, the universe –"

"You feel I'm too stupid."

"I never said that," he laughed in spite of himself, aware that he practically had. Chewing his bite thoughtfully, he decided he might as well. "Ok, let's start with a solar system. I'm sure you're aware we are on a planet."

"Earth."

"Yes, and there are a few others that orbit the sun with us."

"Yes, we've known about other planets for

centuries," she bit tartly, her distaste for his attitude apparent.

"Ok, so let me gather a few trinkets for props." Scooping their blanket off the floor, he dropped it on the couch as he stood before the book case filled with knickknacks. Selecting a few, he carried them back to the table.

In the center, he placed a small statue, and surrounded it with a few others. Indicating one shaped like a small boat, he suggested "This is Earth."

"All right."

"Earth and the rest of the planets do two things. They turn," he lifted and rotated the boat. "This gives us days."

Gwen nodded, fully engrossed in the lesson despite his condescending tone.

"And they revolve around the sun in an orbit, which gives us years." He demonstrated the motion as well.

"So far, my astronomy lessons hold," she grunted with a flare of sass.

"Well, now it gets tricky because this last portion is a few hundred years from being explained."

Her eyes wide, she remained fixed on the objects before her, as if they might begin moving on their own accord at any moment.

Waving his hand out over the scene, he continued, "As you can see, this looks like a perfectly flat system. But it really isn't. All the stars that we see out in the night sky are just like this one." He pointed at the larger statue in the center. "They have planets around then all moving and flowing in their orbits and cycles."

"And they never run into each other?" she gasped.

"Sometimes they do," he agreed, shrugging at her observations. "But the trick is, the suns in the center of these solar systems are not stationary. They are also moving, flying through space away from the center of it." He grabbed the statue and propelled it gently away from the table in a straight line.

"It's leaving us behind?" she asked in awe.

"No. We are still moving around it because of the sun's gravity. It is holding us with it as it flies." He picked up the boat and added the revolutions, following the sun as it moved. "See how we are never quite in the same place twice?"

Standing, she walked around him as he repeated the motion, watching him demonstrate for several minutes. Finally, she concluded, "We are on an endless journey through the cosmos and never in the same point in time and space more than once."

Dropping his hands to his sides, he gaped at her, astonished she would grasp such a concept at her point in history. "Yeah, basically." Placing the Earth and sun back on the table, he looked around, then spied his pencil. Deciding to use it for his final prop, he held it over the earth. "Pretend this is a straw," he commanded.

"A straw? As a piece of hay?"

"No," he grimaced, thinking of an equivalent. "In the future, we have these hollow tubes that we can use to suck things through, like a hose."

"Oh, like a reed."

"Yes, just like that. The center part is hollow, with a starting end and an ending end, where things go in, are trapped inside, and then are released."

"All right."

"The time bubble is like the straw. The special machine we have opens the bubble by poking it through the earth. It has a starting day and an ending day, like the ends of the straw. All the time in between is captured but only as the earth passes exactly through the straw. The rest of the time it is out of line because it's still revolving around the sun. Therefore, inside the bubble, I only experience a fraction of the days that have taken place."

"And as it moves through space, it intersects a different part of the straw, changing the year," she speculated.

Nathan couldn't believe his ears. "There's no way you understand this."

Looking up from the table, she met his wide eyes, hers narrowed with concern. "You claim you do not see me as stupid, but saying things like that will not convince me."

"Honestly, Gwen, I don't know what to make of this. This is a difficult concept, and I can see you have grasped it. Maybe I should have been a physics professor instead," he chortled.

"Perhaps you should have," she clipped, still not amused.

"What are you so angry for? You wanted to know how it worked, and that is exactly it. The only thing I haven't explained is the end."

"When you hit the end of the straw it cuts off and sends you home," she guessed, her voice tight.

"Exactly," he continued to grin. "Gwen, that's amazing. If I didn't know any better, I'd say you didn't belong here." Instant regret twisted his gut as the words he had intended to hold came flying out. He hoped that she had missed his meaning, but she was as sharp as ever.

Her mouth opening slowly, she moaned, "What do you mean I don't belong here?"

Shaking his head with a half grin, he soothed, "Nothing. Not really. I just think you are such a brilliant young woman." He stopped himself there, knowing anything else he might add could not be changed or helped, and the words were better left unspoken; but deep inside, he wondered how the hell she had been born in this century instead of his.

TEN

When the Music Ends

MANOR HOUSE
December 24th, 1797 – year 38

Holding her head high, Gwendolyn stepped from her chamber. Her hair curled, it hung in tight ringlets around her immaculately groomed features. Her dress a floor-length gown, it had been purchased for the evening's ball, one that she had never worn and would never don again. *Christmas is a magical time, for all but me,* she observed, glancing at her image in a full-length mirror in the hall. Her faith in the holiday had waned over the years.

From the outside, she made a presentably beautiful hostess. On the inside, her mind screamed, and any smile curling her lips would be fleeting, forced to hide the turmoil within. She should have spent the day making love to Nathaniel, but that was one mistake she could not afford to make. Her life was crumbling around her, like a sad melody near to reaching its end, and she had no desire to bring Nate down with her.

I've been Geoffrey's plaything for twenty long and grueling years, and I've had enough, she thought as she floated down the corridor to the grand ballroom. The man had fooled everyone, and she had helped him in his cause, covering for his outrageous acts and supporting his scandalous behaviors. *My father would be ashamed if he knew.* Or perhaps he already knew and had chosen to look the other way. As it was, the only person who knew all the details of her life was Nathan, and in a few hours, he would be lost to her forever.

A frown tugging at her lips, Gwen recalled that Alexander had announced only yesterday that he would break with tradition, leaving Astrid Estate to Geoffrey's hands; a shocking turn of events that could tear the family apart. Her brothers had not spoken to her since her arrival, and she knew of their angry disappointment, as their silence spoke volumes. Tonight, she would stand at Geoffrey's side as they formally took possession of the old house that tomorrow would become her new home, and it broke her heart to do so.

Thinking of Nathan as she moved, regret brought tears to her eyes. She knew if she had gone to him, he would have had to drag her out of his cottage. Since she had learned how the magic bubble worked, she had thought of little else. *I could escape.* All she had to do was be inside when the straw reached the end. The bubble would close, and she would be transported with him back to whatever year he came from.

But it wasn't that simple, and she knew it.

There was still a chance no one would know of Nate's transgressions. He had given it his best effort, after all, to remain a good and distant analyst. His broken heart was her fault. He could deny the depth of his feelings, but she felt the love in his hands every time he touched her. He would not escape their time together unscathed even if his superiors never discovered what had transpired between them.

Taking her place next to Geoffrey, she closed her eyes for a moment, allowing her mind to settle. *Christmas had been a magical time for me when I was able to share it with Nathaniel.* The memory of the hours and days she had spent with her lover comforted her, and she knew she only needed to survive one more night. After that, he would get away, swooped back to his time in his magical bubble, and she would deal with what was left of their world; the one they had been building together for her entire life, or so it seemed.

Cottage Outpost
    December 24th, 1797 – year 38

Washing away the residue from his shave, Nathaniel admired his rugged features. He had always seen himself as ordinary with little to offer, but Gwen had given him a new perspective. He had known her scarcely a month, and yet he had shared her entire life.

Tomorrow, she will die, he reminded himself gravely. The how and why tore at him, as the unknown details still remained in the murky darkness of time that could not be seen. He was there to discover them, and the idea of it terrified him.

Selecting a coat from his trunk, he closed the lid with a thud. His heart ached as he prepared to leave, fear gripping him that his choice would hold a finality neither of them could fight. She had decided to forgo their meeting that day. Or had been prevented from keeping it. Either way, he was going to the evening's ball to discern what had become of her.

He didn't have to. He could simply remain in his parlor and perhaps have a nap before the bubble closed. But he had to know. He could not leave this last page of her story unread.

Once he left the cottage, the crisp evening air seemed to reach the depths of his soul. However, instead of freezing him in place, it gave him strength and purity of spirit. He wasn't going to the manor to discover what the cause of Gwendolyn Astrid Romano's death on Christmas Day would be. He was going there to prevent it. Or at least, postpone it if he were able. *This is going to be tricky,* he mused as he navigated the slippery forest floor.

Clearing the trees and taking the familiar path, the lights of the house shone in the distance. The sight brought a smile to his lips, and he whistled to himself as he strolled along, his arms swinging with the lightness of his steps.

In the back of his mind, he thought he should be anxious, even frightened at the course he had decided to take. *Nope.* He wasn't going to back down. For twenty years, he had watched from the sidelines as Geoffrey Romano had abused the woman he loved, torturing her and snuffing the light in her eyes one year at a time. *Tonight, that man is going to pay.*

Arriving at the porch, he climbed the steps, his boots falling silently upon the wooden planks. Reaching for the handle of the door, he could hear the music inside, the festive occasion inviting. *This is it,* he breathed. *No turning back now.*

Inside, the rooms had been decorated in bright red and gold, with ribbons and greenery on the walls and banisters. From the ceiling, a new chandelier hung over the gathering, or at least new to him. Looking around, slightly in awe, it was as if he noticed the magical quality of the evening for the first time in all the times he had been there.

Working his way along the wall, he remained behind the majority of the crowd, his eyes roving over it as he searched. *Come on. Where is she?* His pulse quicker with each minute that passed, he pondered if she were ill somewhere in the house. *In an upstairs bedroom perhaps.*

His eyes silently skimming the incline, they reached the balcony, as if he could look through the walls and see the private chambers above.

"Nate," a soft voice called him back to the present, a small hand resting on his arm.

Pivoting, he looked down to see his angel standing beside him. The relief apparent on his features, his knees almost buckled as he reached for her, then remembered his place and drew back as if her touch had scorched him.

"Might I have a dance?" she asked, offering him the offending hand.

"But of course," he recovered, accepting the appendage and leading her out to the floor.

Taking their turns among the others, his eyes never left her face. "Why didn't you come?" he hissed.

"Not here," she replied with the sweetest grin. "Finish the waltz, and we will retire to a private chamber," she assured.

His nerves raw, it took every ounce of effort he could muster to do so. As they spun, he could see her family members around them. Men and women who had once been young but now wore aged beards and grey hair. *My God, have I really been here this long?*

Spying Douglas, Gwen's eldest brother and ten

years her senior, three young men next to him could be none other than his sons. When their eyes met, Nathan felt a mild stab of panic at the angry glare the eldest Astrid gave him. *Surely, he won't recognize me.* He had stopped coming to the ball before Gwen and Geoffrey's engagement had been announced, and he felt semi-confident that none of those there that night would know him. But what if they did?

The music ended abruptly, and a round of applause sounded around the room before the next song began. Seizing her partner's arm, Gwendolyn led him out through the crowded hall and to a private study. Closing the door gently behind them, a fire illuminated the area around it and little else.

"Well, this is cozy," Nathan observed, the anger replaced with sass. "So, where were you?" he demanded once more.

"I couldn't come," she faltered, lighting candles and lamps around the room.

"You look well. Heck of a time for a sick day," he made the jab, his mind screaming *what the hell are you doing?* at the same time.

"A sick day," she chuckled, not really sure what he meant but certain he was displeased. Satisfied with her task, she turned to face him and offered, "I thought it best if I didn't go there. To that place."

"You went there every year for, oh, two decades. Suddenly it wasn't good enough. Or was I not good enough?" He folded his arms across his chest, causing them to rise and fall with his deep, disgruntled breaths.

Hearing the hurt in his voice, she recoiled. "Oh, Nate, you were always good enough." Reaching out, she laid her hand on his arm. Drawing closer, her mahogany orbs danced with the firelight. "I was afraid of what would happen if I went there. I knew I couldn't go back with you, but I was so tempted to insist that you take me."

Studying her, his jaw dropped. "You want to return with me… to the future?" he asked in a loud whisper, as if the walls might hear his secret.

"Yes, very much so." She sniffed. "I've had all of this life I can stand, I'm afraid, and I'm desperate enough I know I would have guilted you into taking me."

"Guilted me," he parroted, wondering if she knew what tomorrow would bring. Looking her up and down, he repeated, "You look healthy enough. Gwen, I really don't understand." *What if Geoff is finally going to kill her?*

The idea of it wrenched his gut, but not so deeply as his next thought. *What if her death comes because of me?* He would never harm her on purpose, but what wouldn't a man in love do in a fit of rage? *Dear God, this cannot be happening.*

"What does that have to do with anything?" she demanded, her own temper rising. "That's the second time you have mentioned my health. Is something going to happen to me?" She didn't know how far his predictive powers went, but his words at the moment terrified her to the core.

Staring at her, Nate held her gaze, curling his tongue as he considered his words carefully. He had come there with the intention of putting some finality in their goodbye and not the kind that came from simply slipping back into the future. "Gwen," he breathed, his chest tight. "I have something I must share, but the difficulty of hearing it could prove most severe."

"All right. Have your say," she challenged, her gut burning with fear he would deny his love for her.

However, he had no such tidings to give. Instead, he used her hand to draw her nearer, and he whispered, "I came to this time because of you. I chose my dates of arrival and departure based upon a tombstone I found in the graveyard you previously spoke of."

Her brow furrowed, she waited. When he said nothing more, she spat, "That's it? You saw my grandfather's marker and that has brought you here?"

"No, sweetness." He shook his head gently, his mouth dry. "I chose it because I found yours. Tomorrow, you are going to die," he gushed, afraid he would lose his voice before he had finished.

The color drained from her cheeks as Gwendolyn stared at him. "You don't mean that. You could not possibly know," she denied, her words shaky as she fought to breathe.

"I do," he assured, holding her hand to prevent her from pulling away. "At this moment, I fear your prediction will come true and your husband will lay his final blow upon you. I've come to stop him," he added defiantly.

"Oh, Nate, no! It's not Geoff —" She stopped short, realizing what she must confess. Swallowing, she stiffened her resolve. "Tomorrow, if it as you have seen, I will die by my own hand. I have planned it carefully, a rope over the rail about my neck. A simple fall and I will close my eyes for the last time. The last chapter of my life is written, and the final note of my song will be played," she explained, picturing the balcony where she would be found the next day. Seeing the confusion on his features, she shook her head. "I could not bear the thought of another year without you to hold at the end of it."

Tears on his cheeks, he pulled her into his arms. "Oh, my sweet Gwendolyn," he wept. "What the hell are we going to do?" He couldn't let her off herself, no more than he could take her with him. "You know, I only go back if I'm inside the cottage when the bubble collapses. What if we ran away together?"

The suggestion of an alternative she had never considered, she pushed him away to glare at him. "Where would we go that Geoffrey could not find us?"

"I don't know off the top of my head." Nate shrugged. "But with my knowledge of the past, I'm certain we could locate one. We have this brand-new country with so much room to hide in." He grinned, warming to the idea instantly. "We have to get out of here, though. We need to clear out everything we will need from the cabin before the bubble closes and we lose it forever."

ELEVEN

Forbidden Escape

MANOR HOUSE
December 24th, 1797 – year 38

Douglas Astrid scowled as he watched the couple take a turn around the floor. He had seen Nathaniel before, but his brain fuzzy with punch, he couldn't quite place where. Still displeased that his father had chosen to give Gwendolyn and her no-account husband a hall of their own there in the family mansion, he had been partaking of the beverage since the night began.

"You appear in a foul mood," Adam observed as he joined him. The next in line by four years, this Astrid was almost as displeased as his eldest brother.

"Well as I should be," Doug slurred, recalling the night he had carried Gwen up the stairs after her sprain. "Our dear little sister has been given more than her share, I assure you."

"You speak of the house," the other agreed in a quieter voice, leaning towards him to keep their words private. "You have a shorter solution to this dilemma? It will come around to us once more when Geoffrey passes, so why trouble ourselves? He has no heir, and Gwen has reached the end of her fertile years, I am certain," he added deviously.

"Do you wish to wait for another man to age before we share what is rightfully ours?" Douglas barked a laugh, raising his glass to the couple as they disappeared down the hall. "No solution presents itself this evening, but I trust that it will. At the moment I am puzzling to place the gentleman in her company."

"Nathaniel Rigby?"

"Yes!" Doug growled loudly, garnering more attention than he desired.

Shushing him, Adam pointed him towards the front porch. "Keep your voice down, will you? We don't want the entire gathering to hear our words."

"I don't care what is heard," Douglas insisted. "There is something out of the ordinary about our neighbor's visits. I don't think he has changed much since the time I saw him last."

"And?" Adam shrugged, enjoying the cooler air.

"You don't find that strange? A man who is not proper kin attended the ball near twenty years, then disappears for a second twenty. When he returns, there is no discernable difference in his appearance," Doug grunted, leaning against the railing. "You don't find that an oddity?"

Squinting at his older sibling, Adam observed, "Even if he looks the same, he must have aged. Unless you are proposing he is a vampire or some other ghostly figure of sorts." The idea of his brother's misgivings gave him a short fit of laughter. Once it had died away, he suggested, "Let's go have a closer look."

"What sort of look?"

"You know the sort. I think they went to the study. We should have a peek. Perhaps we will catch them in their act of adultery or whatever it is they are doing in there," he insisted.

"What good would that do?" Doug shook his head, not to be bothered with his sister's affairs.

"Well, it might gain us a bit of leverage in keeping her and Geoffrey out of this house. If her husband is not aware of her illicit behavior, it could create a rift in our favor."

Perking up at this last observation, Douglas quickly agreed. "Fine. Lead the way and let us expose their misdeeds."

Fighting their way through the crowded room to the study, the pair opened the door easily. Inside, they found no sign of the couple they had come for. Looking under and behind the furniture, Doug even checked behind the long drapes that hung beside the floor-to-ceiling windows. "This isn't right," he mumbled. "Why would they hide their departure?"

"This I do not know," Adam shrugged. "Wait here," he instructed. Leaving his drunken sibling in the room, he went in search of his father. A man of eighty years, his head had not been clear in some time, and in his second son's opinion, this fact was evidenced by his decision to pass the house to his son-in-law rather than his sons, even if only for a few years.

Locating him in a corner of the ballroom, he glowered at the man next to him as he approached. "Geoffrey," he spat, somewhat less than cordially, as if dismissing him. "Father, I need a word."

"Then have your word," Alexander Astrid countered. "It's Christmas Eve. If not of dire importance, it can wait a few days."

"Very well. Douglas and I believe that Gwen has run off with the Rigby gentleman. They were in the study and have disappeared from the house completely... together." Dropping his final word to leave it hanging in the air, he turned his back to walk away. Geoff caught his arm to negate his departure.

"What gentleman?" her husband demanded gruffly.

"I only know him as Nathaniel. It's been a few years since he has attended, perhaps since you and Gwen were wed. He was here, and they took a turn around the floor. When they finished, they went to the study, but when we went to speak with them, they had departed in a quiet fashion," Adam explained, frowning at Doug who had somehow located him.

"Why did you leave me behind?" his older brother demanded, his inebriated state embarrassing.

Shaking his head, Alex observed, "What a mess our family has become. Drunkards and lay-a-bouts, all of you. If not for Gwen –"

"Gwen is gone, father," Douglas pointed out for the second time.

His eyes scanning the room since the first time her departure was mentioned, Geoffrey had failed to locate her. "I think this bears further investigation. Where might they have gone?"

"She likes to take strolls in the woods," Doug pointed out.

"The woods?" Alex asked doubtful. "She injured herself there a few years back."

"When she was fifteen," Adam pointed out. "Have you forgotten the ball she missed because of her twisted ankle? We never did discover what she was doing at the time."

"She visits the forest every year," Geoffrey observed, his voice deep as he noted the subtle detail he had overlooked in the past. An odd silence fell over the group of men, and he asked in earnest, "You said she has known this man for many years?" Could his wife have been having an affair all this time, with secret rendezvous in the forest? The very thought of such a thing blurred his vision with rage.

"I think we should make a journy to have a look around."

"It's dark out there," Doug suggested. "Be sure you take some light."

"I think we can make do with a few lanterns and perhaps some torches," Alexander offered, still shaking his head at his eldest son.

Locating one of the servants, he was sent to gather the tools while Geoffrey went in search of a few friends. As soon as they had a fair number, the torches and lanterns were distributed, and the group began their trek down the road. It had snowed earlier that day, which would mean with any luck the trail the couple had left behind would be easy to find.

TWELVE

Burning Rage

COTTAGE OUTPOST
  December 24th, 1797 – year 38

Arriving at the cottage after exiting via the back of the house and away from the party, Gwen and Nate began packing the things that might come in handy. "I think I should find a place to spend the night while you go back to the manor," Nathan suggested.

"Why?" Gwendolyn gasped. "I want to stay with you!"

"Yes, I know you do, but no one knows of your intent to leave, and I think it would be wiser to get a full night's start on them. I can pack everything up properly, and we'll work out the details on where we are going to meet, say tomorrow afternoon in the township," he explained. "You can pack your clothes as well, and we will have a proper start on our new life."

"Tomorrow is Christmas," she reminded him tartly while dropping what she had found of his clothes into his trunk and snapping the lid shut.

"Yes, exactly. There won't be many people out and about to see us, don't you think?"

Shaking her head at him doubtfully, she sighed. "I'm really having misgivings about trying to get away or make a life here. Perhaps we should each take a change of clothes and whatever money we have on hand. Anything else is a burden when we need to get as far as we can as quickly as we can," she speculated, indicating the size of his wardrobe alone as evidence.

Glancing around at his collection of supplies, he realized she was probably right. Most would be worthless in survival situations, and it would slow them down to one extent or another. *If we had prepared for this sooner, it would have helped.* In the least, they would need a wagon or carriage and a team of horses to take all that he owned. While he considered her words, he noticed lights in the trees through the large front glass. "Oh no," he groaned.

"What?" she asked, following his gaze. "Oh no."

"I said that," he pointed out, moving to the front door and making sure it was locked. "Douse the lights," he commanded.

"What about the fire?" she asked, extinguishing the candles on the mantle while he took care of the table.

"Leave it. We'll go to the kitchen and hide out of sight. This is the only window, and we wish to avoid being seen." Offering his hand, he gripped hers tightly as they slipped into the other room.

"Do you have any weapons?" she whispered as he placed her in one of the kitchen chairs.

"I'm afraid not," he replied with a shake of his head. "I've never needed one before and have never traveled with one."

"Well, tonight you may need one," she pointed out in dismay.

"Tell me something I don't know." He laughed gently, despite the tension in the air.

Glaring at him, she wondered if he were serious.

Catching the gaze, he chortled a little louder. "It's an expression where I come from." As soon as he said it, they both grinned.

"How long before the time bubble closes?" she asked with a hint of hope in her voice.

"It's dark in here," he observed, pulling the pocket watch out so he could attempt to read it. Turning different directions, he held it up to catch what light filtered into the room. Finally giving up, he sighed, "I don't know. I'd have to go back to the parlor to read it." Snapping it closed, he returned it to his pocket and looked around. "Do you hear them outside?"

"Yes, I believe that I do," she agreed, nodding

at him through the dim light. "What do you suppose they're doing?"

"Probably trying to decide if we are inside, and if they want to bust in to find out."

"Oh. If they don't think we are here, perhaps they will leave us be."

"You said this cottage doesn't exist," he pointed out.

"It's a ruin the rest of the year," she clarified. "They will know something is strange about it."

"Then they will know we are inside, whether they break in or not."

"I think you're right," she agreed, listening to the angry voices muffled by the walls. "Oh my God!" she squealed, pointing at the shadow of dancing flames on the wall. "Are they trying to kill us?"

Fear in her voice, Nate inhaled deeply, then tried to soothe her. "We need to remain calm. They probably think we will come out if we're in here."

"What about the jump?"

"They don't know about that. The question is, will it happen before the house burns down around our ears." Pulling the watch out again, he opened the case and stepped into the foyer. Holding it up, the added light from the fire outside illuminated the small white face. "Five minutes, maybe."

"Maybe? What's maybe?"

"It's about five minutes," he countered, anger creeping into his tone. "I didn't look at the exact time when I arrived, so I guessed the jump times. I'm accurate within five minutes."

"So, if it's five to the guess, we could be looking at ten before it happens."

He shrugged, feeling guilty at the moment. "Ok, yes. Maybe ten if I'm off by five in the wrong direction."

"Nathan, that's terrible!"

"I know," he agreed quietly, the scent of smoke reaching his nostrils. "I would say we could hope the fire is just a scare tactic, but I don't think that it is. I think we should go outside and take our chances with your husband."

"Nate, he'll kill you."

"Maybe." He shrugged again, realizing the option was a poor one. "But what choice do we have?"

"We stay here and hope for the jump," she replied stiffly. Standing to reach him, she took his hand, closing her fingers around his. "I was prepared to hang myself tomorrow, and I'd rather die than live without you," she professed. "If we are going to make it out of this, we do it together."

Her eyes less than a foot from his, he could see her staring up at him. *She's going to die today, all right. In a fire by my side,* he predicted to himself. Flicking his gaze anxiously away, he noted the oversized hearth there in the kitchen, and an excited thrill sent his heart pounding. "That's it! I have an idea," he announced. Dropping her appendage, he grabbed the handles to the large iron pot and lifted it out of the short space. "Man, this is going to be tight."

"What are we going to do?"

"We're going to hide inside of there." He pointed at the small space. "It's fire proof, more or less. All we need is a bit of cover. I'm going to go grab the blankets. With what's left in the vat, we can wet them and cover ourselves."

"But we'll be burned," she protested.

"Maybe," he agreed, leaving her to dart into the parlor. The flames danced high across the window, and he could see the roof had caught. Seizing the coverings, he returned to the kitchen and shoved one of them into the vat. "We have to hurry. The fire is spreading quickly."

Climbing into the ashes on the floor of the fireplace, Gwen squatted and leaned against the back wall. "It feels warm in here."

"Probably. The whole cottage is going to get a lot warmer," he predicted. Using the wet blanket, he covered her with the dripping material. Returning to the vat, he plunged the second in, only to discover the water was all but gone. Hoisting it out, the material was damp at best. "It'll have to do," he muttered as he joined her in the cramped space.

The last thing he remembered was pulling the blanket over himself before the roof caved in and a few of the bricks from the chimney landed on their heads.

THIRTEEN

One Poor Choice

DEPARTMENT OF HISTORICAL Research
  Analyst Control Center
  Eighth Floor Access Chamber
  December 25th, 2084

"Oh my God. What the hell is going on?" Carson Cane shouted when the remnants of a burned building appeared on their terminal pad.

"This is the cottage Nathaniel Crabtree sent out yesterday, or what's left of it," his teammate Andy Harris countered.

"Dear God," Carson moaned, only hesitating for a moment. Turning, he hit the red emergency button on his console and began shouting orders. "We've had an accident in Access Eight," he announced over the PA to alert security and emergency crews. "I need medical crews and a fire team on the double!"

"It's Christmas," Andy pointed out, grabbing a fire extinguisher from the wall and dousing the few flames that remained. "We're on a skeleton crew."

"I know," the floor manager agreed. "We need to tear this down and look for his body. If he's alive, maybe we can still save him."

Coming through the door, the EMTs hustled in, one of them carrying a long board used to transport victims to the med center. Dropping their gear, they immediately began assessing the building's remains to assist with the search.

The fire crew arrived right behind them, the lead shouting, "This material is hot! We need a hose in here."

"I'm on it," his cohort replied, hauling the hose in and opening the nozzle. It took three of them to hold the pressurized hose in line. After a few minutes of cooling what remained, they cut off the flow and began to paw through the rubble by hand. A moment later, the kitchen chimney collapsed to reveal a scorched quilt inside.

"Over here," Andy shouted, spying the contents first.

Converging on the location, the group located Nate as he sprawled over Gwen in an effort to protect her. Lifting him out, they placed him on the stretcher and hauled him out the door, headed for the med center. "Gwen," he coughed in the fresher air of the hall.

"Gwen?" one of the EMT's asked doubtfully. "Wasn't his jump a solo?" he asked the other.

"Gwen," Nathan repeated, his voice weaker.

"I'll run back and have them keep searching," the attending fireman offered, retracing their path. When the doors parted, he could already hear the shouting and called down the hall, "They found her! We're going to need another board in here, stat!"

Department of Historical Research
    Analyst Control Center
    Med Center Recovery
    December 25th, 2084

Aware that he was lying on his back, Nathan could hear the sound of voices; distant, as if they were coming through the walls of the burning cottage. "Gwen," he screamed with a jerk of his prone body. His eyes flicking open, the fluorescent lights above him burned them, and he blinked against the glare.

"Relax, Nate," a voice soothed as a hand rubbed his shoulder. "She's here. She's rough, but the doc thinks she'll pull through."

Rocking his head side to side, the injured man sobbed, "They burned the cottage around us. I thought we were going to die."

"Don't worry about any of that," Paul Hidalgo commanded, approaching his bed from the other side. "There'll be time to explain when you're better."

Recognizing the second man, Nathaniel's heart raced. "I guess I've lost my perfect record, sir. Did my journal make it?"

Glancing at the attendant, Paul laughed, "I can't believe that's what you're worried about. You were minutes away from death, if that much. And as far as the exposé, I'm not going to sugar coat it. You're in trouble and will have a great deal to answer for. At the moment, you need to focus on getting better."

His eyes stung, and Nate blinked them a few times rapidly. "Thank you, sir," he offered aloud. Paul may have been a pain in the ass as far as control agents go, but he had always been fair. *If this was meant to work out, it will,* Nate predicted before he lost consciousness and drifted back into oblivion.

FOURTEEN

A Christmas in Time

DEPARTMENT OF HISTORICAL Research
  Analyst Control Center
  35th Floor Meeting Room
  December 27th, 2084

Sitting in the hall outside the hearing room, Nathaniel and Gwendolyn quietly awaited the verdict on his actions. In the back of his mind, he thought he should keep his hands to himself and think of a story that could get him out of this mess. The rest of him had already decided if his career was over, it was a good run.

Smiling at the woman next to him, he offered his hand. "What do you think so far?" he whispered softly.

"I love it," she giggled, her eyes darting around. They had stayed Christmas night in the med center while they were treated for smoke inhalation but had been released late Christmas day. She had spent last night at his small apartment but had slept little in light of all there was to discover. "I think we made the best choice."

"I have to agree," he informed her with a squeeze of his digits.

A young woman opened the door next to them and beckoned them to enter with a wave of her hand. Inside, a large table held most of the floor space, with a row of five chairs on either side and two on each end. Paul Hidalgo occupied one of those on the far end and nodded firmly as the couple entered.

On the far side, three gentlemen dressed in suits sat in a row, an empty seat between each of them. *Control for control,* Nate surmised, admiring their suits that ranged in color from light grey to black. Nodding at them in greeting, he waited, the girl scooting closer to him with obvious distrust. "It's ok," he soothed, offering her a seat in one of the center chairs on their side of the table. "They only look scary. No one is going to hurt you here."

"Are you trying to be funny?" the man in the darkest suit accused.

"Oh, no sir," Nathan grinned, realizing letting go had afforded him a great deal of peace in the process. "We've just survived a fire, and she was physically and mentally abused before that, so she's a little skittish if you know what I mean."

Turning the disgruntled glare to the woman, the spokesman of the board studied her. "What's your name, ma'am." His dark clothing made a formidable impression on the girl's nerves.

"Gwendolyn Margaret Astrid Romano," she supplied dutifully, her voice surprisingly strong to Nates ears.

"What year were you born?" the questions continued.

"Seventeen sixty," she admitted with a doleful glance at the man next to her.

"I think this is an open and shut case," the second gentleman in the lightest grey suit stated loudly.

"Uh, if I could interrupt for just one moment, I have one thing I think you should see before you make up your minds," Paul offered from the far end of the table, speaking for the first time.

Standing, Nate's control agent presented a copy of the same picture to both sides of the table, one to Nathan and Gwen, and the second to the row of gentleman on the other side.

Glancing down at the image, Nate ran his hand roughly over his face. "Don't you think she's been through enough?" he demanded, glaring at the man who had presented the evidence.

"Would you like to know what that is?" Paul asked with a hint of mystery in his voice.

"I would," Gwen whispered, her finger tracing the edges of her headstone. "Is this why you came to Astrid Estate?" she asked, addressing the man beside her.

"You could say that," he shrugged. "I included this in my travel request to support my need for an extended stay." Meeting the eyes of the men across from him, he waited for the hammer to fall.

"Actually, that's not exactly what this is," Paul countered, his words even more cryptic. "That is a snapshot I took of her headstone this morning. I hunted for it yesterday and had to get one of the historians from the local chapter to help me locate it."

Snatching up the photo, Nate glared at it. *December 25, 1797.* Fumbling in his inner pocket, he pulled out is personal device and called up the request he had submitted before his trip was approved. Quickly skimming to the last page, he dropped the mini-computer on the table and turned to look at the woman next to him. "They look the same. They thought we died in that fire and gave you a grave."

"How do you know these images didn't change with the alteration of the timeline?" the lead interviewer asked.

"I don't." Nate shrugged. "But I know for a fact that's the day she died before. It's the whole reason I scheduled my flight when I did," he confessed.

"And you are certain of this?" Paul pushed.

"Absolutely," Nathan chuckled. "And I can tell you now, I'm not sorry for bringing her back with me. Truth be told, if her family hadn't burned the house down around us, I had intended to gather a few things and disappear in seventeen-ninety-seven."

"You mean her family did this?" the medium

grey suit asked incredulously. Holding up a picture of the mess left in the access chamber, he appeared shocked at the revelation.

"Well, her husband. And her father, I think," Nate presumed.

"And my brothers. I'm sure they helped." Gwen sighed.

"I don't think this is an open and shut case after all," Paul added.

Staring at him, Nathan couldn't believe his control seemed to be standing up for him. "Thank you, sir."

The spokesman tried again. Presenting a large plastic bag, the remains of Nate's field journal had been stored inside. The delicate pieces of paper charred and the cover severely damaged, only a portion of their careful recordings remained. "Are you willing to take an oath or a lie detector test as to the validity of this manifest?"

"I'll take or do anything you like because what's in there is the truth," Nathan grinned. "I have nothing to hide here. I know what I did was against policy and falls under the category of professional misconduct, and I'll accept whatever punishment comes of that. I don't regret it, and if either of those things cost me my job, then I guess I'm in the market for a new line of work."

"Actually," the light grey suit spoke up, "I have something else I think we should consider. I'd have to pull the case file, but I'm certain that this situation has happened before. A time lock, I believe it was referred to."

"Happened before?" Paul asked in surprise, unsure how that would be possible.

"Not this exact chain of events, but we did have an instance recorded where the actions of the analyst should have caused a ripple effect in the timeline, but upon examination, none could be traced. I'm almost certain this is what has happened here," he suggested confidently. "It's as if a circle of events has occurred, like a repeating loop of cause and effect."

"So, what you're saying is that I did what I was supposed to do? Because things turned out the way they had been?" Nathan asked, his face scrunched in an odd manner.

Picking up the photo of the headstone again, the foreman curled his fingers at Nate. "Let me see your shot of the headstone."

Standing, the analyst offered him the device across the large, flat surface between them. Laying them both side by side, the group of three leaned in closer to study them together. "These are not the same," the dark grey suit observed, enlarging the image from Nate's device. "Look at these edges. The dates and information match, and the carving is standard for the era. But the stones themselves are not identical."

"What do you mean?" Gwen asked anxiously, still not entirely sure what to make of their proceedings.

"These stones are made of sandstone," the light grey suit explained. "No matter how careful you are, they are never identical over time. There is too much variation within the pieces of stone itself. They will weather differently even under identical conditions. Therefore, we can only conclude that you were declared deceased on Christmas Day, regardless of what took place while Mr. Crabtree was there. You died in both timelines, and the present remained unaltered. This is definitely a time lock."

"We'll want to study this instance further," their third member observed. "I'll open a case file with the department of mechanical studies."

"I'm good with that," the foreman agreed, tapping the picture with a stiff finger, then pointing it at the couple across from him. "We'll consider where you will be assigned, but I'm confident your position can be preserved, and we will likely need more input from both of you as the research unfolds. But I guarantee, you get in the least amount of trouble again, and no amount of evidence is going to help you."

"Yes, sir." Nathan laughed nervously, breathless that the decision had fallen in his favor.

"What about me?" Gwen asked quietly.

Smiling at her, Nate held up his hands. "All my research notes are as good as destroyed, so I guess if you want your story shared, you'll need to help me write the exposé."

"You mean, you're still going to tell it?" she gasped.

"Why wouldn't I?" He sighed, reaching for her hand. "As I said to Paul before I left, yours is a tale that simply has to be told."

"So, I guess there really is Christmas magic," she beamed, her eyes flicking around with pure joy at finally having the home she had always dreamed of.

"Oh," Nathan grunted, surprised by the notion. He had spent his whole life denying the existence of a higher power, or any power for that matter that couldn't be explained by science. Uncomfortable, he inhaled deeply, then released the air slowly through his nose.

On the table before him lay the picture of a gravestone, the one that had caught his attention months ago. Picking it up with his free hand, he studied it with a distant glaze over his eyes. *I built my whole mission around this,* he silently mused. Staring at the final date, *December 25th*, he could not deny the significance of it. "Do you really believe it's magic?" he asked in a subdued tone.

"What I believe doesn't matter," Gwen whispered in return. "I only know I wished for you long before I knew who you really were. My true love came to me every Christmas Eve and helped me escape to a new and better life. It doesn't get any more magical than that."

About the Author

Anyone who knows me could tell you, I am a friendly kind of person, never met a stranger and take up conversations anywhere at any time. I work hard, and my mind never seems to shut down, as I wake up often in the middle of the night with ideas pouring out and demanding to be dealt with. Of course that means much of my books were written in the middle of the night.

I grew up and still live in the great state of Texas where everything is bigger, where we have warm weather and a central location. I love my state, my town, and my family, which includes my four sons, my significant other, and many friends as well.

I have thoroughly enjoyed writing this story and hope that you will love reading it just as much. And of course, there will be many more adventures to come.

You can follow Samantha Jacobey at:
Website: **www.SamJacobey.com**
Facebook:
https://www.facebook.com/SamJacobey
Twitter: **https://twitter.com/SamJacobey**

Also by SAMANTHA JACOBEY

A New Life Series – an epic adventure, TORI FARRELL's life IS one wild story... escaped from a biker gang and running from drug lords... used by the FBI and hoping to protect her present from her past... IT'S DARK - IT'S BRUTAL, and it's WORTH EVERY MINUTE OF IT!! (Mature read, 18 ⊦ for graphic sexual content and violence, including rape)

Summer Spirit Novella Series - no one EVER had a summer romance like this... Charlie visits another plane, parallel to our own, where Summer Angels and Dark Angels battle over the fate of man. A unique twist on an old idea that will keep you guessing; will Charlie and Clarisse ever find their HEA? (New adult)

Irrevocable Series – Armageddon through the eyes of an entitled seventeen-year- old, BAILEY DEWITT's life has become a broken mess... after her parents died unexpectedly, she didn't think it could get any worse. But when the arrogance of man catches up and puts the entire world into a dooms-day spiral, there will be only one place she can run to - the one place she wanted desperately to escape. Can she and Caleb build a life together when the world is falling apart? (New Adult)

Teach Me to Prey – in this standalone thriller, JASON TRUITT and his friends have gotten their way for years. Deceit, sex, and foul play aren't normally covered in the curriculum, but they're doing whatever it takes to get under BECKY STEWART's skin. When one of the boys turns up dead, it's a race against time to save the others; a STUNNING STORY that will get your heart racing and leave you breathless by the end… (New Adult)

The Binding (Unexpected Magic #1) - One cursed diary will change two strangers forever...Can Meri and Rider use her mother's old book to figure out why someone is after them? Or will the guilty party succeed, ripping the tome away before killing them and then slithering back into the darkness… (New Adult)

The Wicked Awakened (Unexpected Magic #2) – a Halloween novel; a five-hundred-year-old witch wants to turn SARAH MATTHEWS' body into her new home… A twisted tale involving a coven hell bent on seeing that she succeeds. Who will come out on top in this epic battle of wills? (Mature read, 18+ for graphic sexual content and violence)

Sweet Christmas Series - Life isn't always sweet, even for girls called Candy. Candice Parker's life has never been easy. Plagued by losses and setbacks, each day is a struggle for the petite brunette and her young son. When fireman Gary enters her world, he is one mistake she refuses to make; but after tragedy strikes, she may not have a choice. (New Adult)

The Dragon of Eriden Series - Amicia Spicer led a simple life, until she discovered it had all been a lie… On her deathbed, Arely Spicer confessed to her only daughter that she had been found by, not born to her mother and father. Sad news to be certain, the idea of having a family of flesh and blood waiting to be reunited sent the young, independent woman on the adventure of a lifetime. Little did she know, a dragon's heart beat within her chest and her journey would be more perilous than she could have imagined... (New Adult)

Also from the Lavish family

Fairfield Corners Series
L.A. Remenicky
http://myBook.to/FairfieldCorners

Small town romance with a paranormal twist!
Each in standalone style, read and enjoy any
order, any number!

Saving Cassie – Book 1: Some secrets are too
dangerous to keep. After ten years in the big city,
Cassie Holt is back in Fairfield Corners. She may
look like the same girl who left home a decade
before but she's hiding a dark truth from everyone. When her life is threatened by the demons of
her past, her best friend—who happens to be the
local sheriff—offers his help. Deputy Logan
Miller has been burned by love. He's not looking
to get involved but duty calls when the sheriff
tasks him with Cassie's protection. Thrown into

close quarters with the gorgeous bookseller, sparks fly. Logan is drawn to Cassie, but it's hard to get close to someone who keeps themselves guarded all the time. To keep Cassie safe, Logan must open his heart but that's something he swore he'd never do.

Ragan's Song – Book 2: One look into his eyes told her she was in trouble – againRagan returned home to celebrate her parent's anniversary hoping they would forgive her the secrets she's kept from them over the last few years. When she discovered that Adam was still living in Fairfield Corners she hoped her secrets were safe, secrets that drove her away three years, secrets that could change both their lives forever. Adam Bricklin was devastated when Ragan Newlin left town. No note, no email, no text. She was just gone. It has taken three years for Adam to finally move past the heartbreak he suffered when Ragan left town. Now he's moved on and everything was going well until the day Ragan returned to Fairfield Corners. Now the melody that he lost all those years ago is back. It's the same tune he heard that tells him right from wrong—the one that sang Ragan was the one. Even separation can't silence Adam and Ragan's song, and now that she's back it's time for Adam to decide if he should let the song die or breathe life into it once again.

Where There's Faith – Book 3: A past she can't remember. A love he can't forget. After losing everything in an accident that he can only blame himself for, Robbie Newlin embraced sobriety and tried to live his life quietly alone at this family's cottage on the lake. Grief being his only ally, Robbie was perfectly content with how he lived until Faith moved into the cottage next door. Now Faith had him questioning whether to keep grieving or to open his broken heart to let love in again. Faith McMillan had no memory of her life before that day three years ago. The physical scars had faded but the emotional ones were still fresh and raw. Living rent-free seemed like a great way to finish her second book and give her the time to figure out her next move, but then she met the reclusive guy next door and everything changed. To get past the broken parts, Robbie and Faith must figure out if they want to continue living their lives in solitude or take a chance on finding an ending together.

The City: The Jane Harvest
A. Nicky Hjort
http://myBook.to/TheJaneHarvest

A dystopian thriller... welcome to the future, or at least one possible future...

Winning battles means Ink honors, prestige, and life itself. ...Yet nobody understands what losing truly means.

On another planet two hundred years in the future, twenty-one-year-old Isla Jane struggles helplessly to figure out who she is and what her world really means. Marked with a forbidden tattoo of the rising sun, she is a natural champion of humanity and a gifted warrior in Heats– lavish battles fought in the conjoined minds of the participants for the morbid amusement of the masses.

Despite Isla's desire to fade into the background, she emerges as an obvious leader of her people when the senseless assassination of a youth forces her to face the truth. Her volatile world, disguised by its elaborate battles and constant mayhem, is a prison without bars and a coffin, the lid already half-closed, that they must escape.

But when she vows to find a way to bring her people back home, Isla will have to deconstruct consciousness and the very nature of the space time continuum to unravel good from evil, truth from lies, and survival from true love.

Welcome to the City—where it takes lives to save lives…